Hardback - ISBN: 978-1-923567-21-4
Paperback - ISBN: 978-1-923567-22-1
eBook - ISBN: 978-1-923567-23-8

Cover design by **Holly Symons**
First Edition

For More, Please Visit

HollySymons.com.au

Aurelya & Loki: The Erasure Prophecy

- Book Four: The Rewrite War,
- Book Five: The War of the Unwritten,
- Book Six: The Library That Eats Endings

&

Books 7–8: *Chaos, Comedy, and the Crown*

Book Four
The Rewrite War

Chapter One: The Baby, The Coma, and The Beginning That Wasn't

A baby cried in a world that hadn't been written yet.

She wasn't born, she was typed. Her heartbeat synced with a blinking cursor. And when her eyes opened, they glowed the colour of red ink.

Not blood.
Correction.

Across the Realms, things were… off.

Tiny things.
Forgettable things.
- A missing page number in a scholar's tome
- A word that flickered in and out of a bard's ballad
- A comma that moved

And only one person noticed:
Aurelya.

She woke up mid-sentence.
Literally.

There was no dream, just text unravelling in her mind.

"Loki," she gasped, "someone's… rewriting while we're still living."

He blinked awake beside her, half-draped in a velvet cape and half in a pillow fort shaped like a llama.

"Is it me?" he asked. "I've rewritten a few moments. Like my taxes. And that unfortunate moment with Thor and the haunted butter churn."

"No. This is different. This is outside us."

The chicken pecked a message into the floorboards.

It read:
"PAGE 197 IS MISSING "

Meanwhile… in the House of Eternal Drafts, Veylion paced the edge of a reality leak.

He could hear echoes from books that didn't
exist anymore.
And in one… he heard Aurelya's name.

Spelled wrong.

"They're tampering with identity," he growled.
"This isn't a rewrite.
This is an overwrite."

Back at the Folded Edge,
a whisper reached the First Flame bearer.

One sentence only:

"The child is here."

She dropped her lantern.

"Not again," she whispered.

And far, far away, in a realm no longer counted
among the Ten…
The baby sat up in her crib.
No one had taught her how.
She looked around.

Then, in perfect handwriting,
she carved a word into the air:

"EDIT."

Let's crack open Chapter Two!
*Time to send Aurelya & Loki sleuthing through
glitchy Realms, whispering shadows, and
suspiciously cheerful NPCs.*

Chapter Two: The Glitch That Smiled Back

It started with a squirrel.

Not their squirrel.

A different squirrel.

This one wore tiny pants and a monocle.
He greeted Aurelya and Loki in the middle of an ancient marketplace and chirped:

"Greetings, travellers! I'm Gliffin, and I've always been here!"

Aurelya and Loki exchanged a look.

"No, you haven't," said Aurelya.

"Of course I have," said Gliffin, with the smooth confidence of a memory recently edited.
"I've been a beloved local character since Book One!"

"We never had a Book One," Loki muttered.

The market shimmered.

A cart turned into a bakery. Then a theatre. Then a goat.
A woman's dialogue reset mid-laugh.
A child walked backward out of a memory.

Aurelya leaned close to Loki.

"We're in a patchwork timeline. Someone's blending rejected drafts into our reality."

"So it's like fanfiction," Loki whispered. "But if the fan had authority and a god complex."

They started checking the seams.

Literally.

They found:
• A town mayor who stuttered between three different accents
• A prophecy wall that changed every time you blinked
• A man named Kevin who didn't remember being a dragon last week

"This place is fractured," Aurelya said. "But the edits aren't stable."

"Sloppy authoring," Loki said. "Someone's rushing to take control."
"Or learning."
Then, they found the message.

It wasn't written; it was folded into the spine of a book that had never existed.

"I am not the Author.
I am the Inheritor.
And I will do what he couldn't:
Finish the story properly."

A chill passed through Aurelya.

"Someone's trying to write us out."

And that's when a new character stepped into view.

A girl.
Red cloak.
Glowing eyes.

And she spoke one word:

"Rewrite."

And suddenly, the entire market collapsed, not in fire, not in rubble,
but in deletion.

One blink...
And it was as if it had never existed.

Next: Into the Prophecy's ashes we go.
Let's uncover the truth *they tried to burn.*

Chapter Three: The Burned Page

In the smouldering ruins of the deleted market, something remained:

A single scrap of parchment.

Blackened at the edges.

Still warm.

Still whispering.

It clung to Veylion's claws when he tried to brush it away.

"It wants to be read," he said, voice low.

Aurelya held it carefully.

The page trembled like a frightened animal.

Then it began to write itself… backwards.

In ink the colour of dried blood.

"When the child names the nameless, the named shall fade."

"When the flame burns backwards, memory shall rot."

"And when the pen falls silent… she will rise."

"What does that mean?" asked Loki.

"It means the baby is the weapon and the author," Aurelya whispered.

"She doesn't need to be taught. She just needs to remember."

"Or be told what to remember," Veylion growled. "That's how you make a god."

Suddenly, the burnt page curled in on itself and sang.

Not a melody.

A single line on repeat:

"Page 274… Page 274… Page 274…"

"We don't have a Page 274," Aurelya said.

"Exactly," Loki muttered. "We've reached the part of the book that's still being written… by someone else."

Veylion raised his head.

"There's only one place that would keep an unnumbered page like that…"

"Where?" asked Aurelya.

"The Realm of Intention," he said.

"What's that?" asked Loki.

"Where stories are born... before they're written."

Chapter Four: Page 274

They found it in the oldest library in the Ten Realms
a place no longer shown on maps and technically burned down three books ago.

It was called The Archive of Almost.

Where every story that almost happened… still whispered.

"This place gives me indigestion," Loki muttered, brushing cobwebs off a scroll titled The Time Thor Became a Sea Turtle (For Reasons).

"Stay focused," Aurelya said.

Then they saw it.

A single page.
Pinned to a wall with no book around it.
Numbered clearly in the corner:

274

Written in red ink.
The script shifted as they looked at it, part prophecy, part threat, part diary entry.

Page 274: The Forgotten Draft

"They think I am a child."

"They think I do not know who they were
before."

"But I see it. I feel it. The Realms are soft clay and
I… I remember the shape they used to be."

"I am not new."

"I am the correction."

"She's not being controlled," Aurelya whispered.
"She's choosing this."

"Worse," said Loki.
"She might believe she's saving us."

At the bottom of the page… a signature:

- N.

"N…?" Aurelya asked.

Veylion stepped forward slowly.

"There was a draft. Years ago. Before any of us
were born."

"A daughter," he said quietly.
"To The Author."

"Her name was Nyra."

Suddenly, the air went ice cold.
The lights dimmed.

And behind them… a voice.

Childlike.
Powerful.
Calm.

"Why are you reading my page?"

They turned.

Standing there… in the dark…

The girl.

Except now she looked… older.

Not just in body.
In presence.

Like she'd aged through memory.

And in her hands?
A quill made of glass and bone.

"I want to show you," she said softly.

"Show us what?" Aurelya asked.

Nyra smiled.

“Your alternate endings.

Chapter Five: The Girl Who Wasn't Meant to Be

The library was gone.

Not collapsed.
Not burned.

Just… gone.
As if someone had hit backspace on a building.

Aurelya stood in the empty space where Page 274 had whispered.
But her mind was elsewhere.

The vision still clung to her memory
the child's realm,
the drawings,
the shadow caretaker,
and that hug…

She could still feel the tiny arms around her waist.
Still hear the words:

"I didn't know."

And deeper than that a truth that shook her:

Nyra didn't ask to be written.

"I think she's just a kid," Aurelya whispered.
"A scared, brilliant kid."

Loki sat cross-legged beside her, chewing on a ghost quill like it was a celery stick.

"A scared, brilliant kid with the power to erase us all."

"Exactly. She's not the villain."

"She's the final draft."

Veylion paced nearby, wings twitching.

"She's not stable," he said.
"She's a patchwork of discarded lore, half-truths, and projected vengeance."

"So was I," Aurelya said softly. "So were you."

Silence.

Suddenly, the wind shifted.

It didn't blow it inhaled.

Like a world holding its breath.

A new line etched itself into the sky.

Carved in red light, high above the Realms:

"THE FINAL VERSION BEGINS NOW."

Nyra had made her decision.

And she wasn't asking permission.

Aurelya turned to Loki.

"We're not just fighting for the Realms."

"We're fighting for her soul."

And from deep below the cracked foundation of
the erased library,
a new staircase began to grow upward.

Page 275 was being written.
And it was calling them down.

Up Next: the forbidden page
the page that shouldn't exist…
and yet somehow does.

Chapter Six: The Silence That Shouldn't Have Been

They were standing on the edge of the Realm of Intention,

where thought hadn't become reality yet

just shapes of things trying to be born.

The air shimmered with fragments of story.

Sentences floating mid-air.

Unspoken dialogue.

Half-finished characters pacing like ghosts.

The lion growled softly.

Not out of fear.

But like it sensed something was watching them... from behind the curtain of the plot.

"What is it, boy?" Aurelya asked.

He looked back at her

and for the first time in all their lives together...

he didn't smile.

Then, it happened.

No flash. No scream. No noise.

Just absence.

Like a candle blown out mid-thought.

One blink.

He was gone.

"No," Aurelya whispered. "No, no, no"

She spun.

The space he had been standing in was still warm.

Loki reached out and touched the air.

It shivered.

"That wasn't erasure," he said.

"Then what?" Aurelya's voice cracked.

Loki looked at the space again.

"That was… a placeholder."

"He's waiting to be written back in."

They looked up.

Above them, high in the sky of the unformed realm:

A single line of glowing red ink scrawled itself across the sky:

"Only the ending can bring back what was lost."

Aurelya took a step forward… and stopped.

Because at her feet…

the dragon was staring at her.

And it was crying.

One tear, molten silver.

"We finish this," Aurelya said softly, "and we bring them all home.

Chapter Seven: The Echo That Never Came Back

They were walking again.

This time, deeper into the Realm of Intention.
Where ideas formed like weather, and time rewrote itself mid-thought.

Loki was rambling.

"You know, if I were a cosmic editor trying to erase us, I'd start with the goat.
No one respects a goat."

Aurelya chuckled.
Even the dragon made a low amused rumble.

"Then again," Loki continued, "maybe they'll go for me.
Iconic. Complicated. Loved and hated in equal measure"

He stopped mid-step.

Mid-word.

Aurelya turned.

And all that remained was:
- One boot
- A single floating comma
- And the smell of ink and apples

"Loki?" she said quietly.

No reply.

The comma fell.
The boot turned to dust.

"NO," she snapped, louder now. "LOKI!"

Nothing.

Not a sound.
Not even a trick.
And then… a whisper.
Not from Loki.

From the Realm itself.

"The Trickster has been shelved for future use."

Aurelya dropped to her knees.

The dragon nudged her with its nose.

In the distance, glowing in the sky like prophecy
graffiti:

"The closer you get to the end, the more alone
you must become."

She stood slowly.

Wiped her face.

"You're not gone," she whispered. "You're just…
between lines."
And then she took her first step forward.
Alone.

Chapter Eight: The Rewrite That Broke the Pen

The Realm of Intention had thinned to parchment.

Aurelya could see the edges of the book now, not metaphorically. Literally.

Blank pages waited beyond the horizon, fluttering in a wind made of plot holes.

She walked in silence. Her dragon kept pace.

Every so often, she'd see echoes of characters who had been written… then cut.

They nodded at her. Some saluted. Some cried.

At the center of it all, a desk.

Ancient. Wooden. And glowing faintly with a pulse she felt in her own chest.

On the desk: a single quill.

Made of a Phoenix feather. Burning, yet eternal.

And beside it... the Final Page.

Aurelya sat.

She took the quill.

And for a moment, she just breathed.

"I'm not the Author," she whispered.

"But I've lived the story."

Then she wrote:

'Let what was lost be returned.'

And with that, the page caught fire in reverse.

From its edges inward, memory returned.

The lion's roar echoed in the sky.

Loki's laughter filled the air, followed by a sarcastic, 'Took you long enough.'

Even the chicken crowed.

Aurelya smiled.

The Realms didn't need a god to fix them.

They just needed someone who remembered how it felt to be broken.

She stood.

The Final Page fluttered once… then vanished.

The pen cracked.

Not out of weakness. Out of completion.

And far, far above the stars reformed themselves into new constellations.

Not names.

Not legends.

But moments.

The story wasn't over.

It never would be.

But this chapter… was complete.

Chapter Nine: The Final Rewrite

The pen hovered in her hand like it already knew what to write.

Aurelya stood in the centre of the unformed chamber no dragon, no Loki, no lion.

Just her.

And silence.

The Pen of Intention pulsed once.

Then... began to bleed.

Ink not black, but gold.

Memory not thought.

The air trembled.

Reality asked her one question:

"**What is your final sentence? **"

Aurelya raised the pen.

Her hands shook.

She could write anything:

- A reset

- A resurrection

- A revenge

- A realm with no gods at all

But what she whispered was:

**"Bring them home." **

And then… she wrote.

The moment the ink touched the air; the chamber shattered like glass.

Not destruction transformation.

Each piece became:

- A door

- A name

- A memory returned

The lion roared back into being, his mane glowing like the first dawn.

The dragon curled around her, silent but whole.

And then, she heard it...

**"Took you long enough." **

Loki stood in the doorway of a new page,

dusting off ink-smudged trousers and twirling an apple like he'd never left.

"You were between lines," she said.

"I was waiting for your comma," he winked.

Then the ground shifted.

Not in fear.

In release.

Across the Realms:

- Characters remembered

- Stories restored

- Pages rewritten, not erased

Aurelya looked down at the pen.

It was no longer glowing.

It had done its job.

And quietly… it turned to dust in her hand.

Veylion appeared beside them.

"There's still one thing left," he said.

"What?" she asked.

He pointed to the sky.

Where one last sentence had appeared:

*"And then they rewrote the ending together." *

Chapter Ten: The Last Rewrite

There was no fanfare.
No drumroll.
No fireworks of fate.

Just a girl.
Holding a pen.

And a blank page.

Nyra stood at the edge of all stories.
Every version, every draft, every note that had
ever been made.
They hovered behind her like ghosts.

The dragon and lion were gone.

Loki was gone.

Even the flame inside Aurelya felt faint.
"You don't have to do this alone," Aurelya
whispered.

Nyra looked at her.
"I already did."

The girl raised the pen.

The world held its breath.

And she began to write:

"This time… no gods."
"This time… no chosen ones."
"This time… everyone matters."

Reality glitched.

The words etched into the stars.
The broken timelines healed like mended paper.
The realms fused not into perfection, but into
possibility.
Aurelya felt the page shift beneath her feet.

She wasn't being erased.
She was being rewritten… with consent.

Loki reappeared first.
Mid-monologue.

"...and that's why goats should unionize."

He blinked.

"I'm back?"

The lion roared.

The dragon cried.

And the stars... clapped.

Nyra fell to her knees.

The pen dropped.

And a final sentence wrote itself into the page:
"In the end, the story chose hope."

Aurelya stepped forward, lifted the girl in her arms.

"It's over," she whispered.

"No," said Loki, smiling softly.

"It's just the last rewrite."

Chapter Eleven: Teamwork Makes the Dream Work, Babe

(Because even a goddess can't rewrite fate alone.)

The Pen of Intention was in Aurelya's hand.

But it was never meant to be held alone.

"You're not the villain," she said, turning to Nyra. "You're the version someone else tried to force into place."

"And you…" she looked at Loki. "You're the reason I remember how to laugh when I should be crumbling."

"I'm the punctuation in your plot arc," he smirked.

She stepped up to the blank page.

Nyra stood across from her.

Loki beside her.

The lion circled back, slow and solemn.
The dragon landed behind them, tail curling into
the shape of a question mark.

"This isn't about winning," Aurelya said.
"It's about writing the kind of ending worth
surviving for."

And then she reached out…

And Nyra did too.

They touched the pen.

Together.

Lines exploded from the page like constellations
finding their place in the sky.

The Realms breathed.
The erased were restored.
The forgotten were remembered.

Thor returned mid-chicken joust.
The squirrel popped out of Loki's hood.
Odin, somehow, was still in the tree.

"I WAS GONE FOR TEN CHAPTERS WHAT DID I MISS?!"

The final page began to settle.

It didn't say The End.

It said:
"This version was written by many hands."
"And it finally feels like home."

TEAMWORK MADE THE DREAM WORK.

Epilogue: The Quiet Between Ink and Fire

The stars looked calm again.

The sky no longer flickered with glitching glyphs.
The rivers flowed forward.
Chickens stopped tap dancing mid-sentence.

For now… the Realms breathed.

Aurelya sat with her legs dangling off the edge of the world.

Below her, clouds shaped like lions and dragons drifted slowly past.

Beside her, Loki appeared in his usual fashion sideways, grinning, holding a snack that absolutely did not exist a moment ago.

"So… we won. Again. Temporarily. Probably."
He offered her half of a peanut butter scone.
"Want to not talk about the existential threat on the horizon and pretend everything's fine for five minutes?"

She smiled. Took the scone.
Let herself lean into the silence.

The lion snored behind them, curled around the
dragon like punctuation.

Nyra slept nearby, surrounded by books she
wasn't reading just... listening to.

Thor was arm-wrestling a dwarf.
Odin was still muttering prophecies into a wine
bottle.
The squirrel had stolen someone's crown and
declared himself King of Snacks.

Everything was beautifully wrong in all the right
ways.

Until the wind changed.

Aurelya sat up straight.

So did the dragon.

So did Nyra.

The lion opened one golden eye and growled.

In the distance... a single page floated across the
sky.

It was black.
Burned around the edges.
The ink shimmered with refusal.

It landed gently at Aurelya's feet.

Loki picked it up, turned it over, and read the
single line aloud:

"I remember what you erased."

Aurelya didn't speak.
She couldn't.

Because the page in Loki's hand began to bleed
new lines before their eyes not written by any of
them.

A new voice had entered the story.

A voice that was once silenced.
And now?
It was writing itself back in.

AURELYA & LOKI

THE WAR OF THE UNWRITTEN

Chapter One: The Page That Shouldn't Exist

It started with a memory Aurelya didn't own.

She stood in the Vault of Final Drafts, where no one was supposed to go without invitation.

The Pen of Intention hovered in its glass case, glowing softly... but not for her.
Not this time.

She stared at the page in her hand, the one Loki had found.
It was still writing itself, line by line.

But not in gold.
Not in crimson.
In ink so black it refused to reflect the light.

And the lines it wrote were personal.

"You rewrote your world at the cost of mine."
"You sealed me in a footnote and called it mercy."

"You don't get to be the hero. Not in my book."

"Loki…" Aurelya whispered.

But he wasn't next to her anymore.

He was there one second, smirking.

Gone the next.

No sound. No flash. Just… removed.

Like a deleted sentence.

She turned.
Nyra? Gone.
The lion? Vanished mid-step.
Even the dragon's warmth was erased, as if the
story had never needed her fire.

Only Aurelya remained
Holding the page.
Surrounded by silence.
The Pen of Intention cracked its own case.

It floated toward her… and turned away.

Rejected.

“You don’t get to write this chapter,” a voice
echoed from the shelves.

It was soft.
Precise.
The kind of voice that had waited too long.

From the shadowed arch between worlds, a
figure stepped out.

They wore words like armour, torn pages for
sleeves, ink across their cheeks.

And in their hand:
The Pen of Obsidian.
Not created.

Not earned.
Stolen.

“Chapter One,” they said, stepping into the centre

of the Vault.
"The Reclaiming."

Aurelya stood frozen.
Not with fear.
But with recognition.

Because the voice didn't belong to a stranger.

It belonged to a version of her that should never
have survived.

Secret Chapter: AUREXIA

(The Chapter That Wasn't Supposed to Exist)

(Hidden between Chapters 1 and 2 of Book Five, on a page sealed with stardust and betrayal.)

Before she was erased,
before she became the villain in the footnotes...
She was the first spark.

They called her Aurexia Flameborn.
Not gentle.
Not patient.
Not polite.

She was a weapon designed by the Tree of Realms itself,
to burn lies,
expose corruption,
and carve truth into the bones of tyrants.

The lion who stood beside her then had no name,
because names are for those allowed to survive
the edits.

The dragon was smaller. Fiercer. Wilder.
And it spoke in prophecy, not flame.

She loved Loki.

Not in passing,
not in hints,
but with the raw, chaotic love of a wildfire.

And Loki?

He chose her.

Until he didn't.

The Rewrite

When the Scribes of the 4th Realm gathered to
"refine" the narrative, they said:

"She's too intense."
"Readers won't relate."
"Give her more vulnerability. Less flame."

"Make her… sweeter. Like a cinnamon scroll that
cries."

They took her pages.
They cut her down.
They rewrote her as Aurelya.

"You were born from my redacted ashes,"
Aurexia whispers now.
"You're not the main character, you're the
replacement."

They left her in the Vault of Abandoned Drafts,
a place where the stories scream when no one's
looking.

And for years, she couldn't write.
Not a word.

Until one day…
a page from the living Realms bled through the
cracks.

And she read about the new Aurelya.

Her softness.
Her hope.
Her Loki.

That was the day Aurexia stole the Pen of
Obsidian.

The day she made a vow:

"They will remember me.
Or I will erase every version of them."

Now, she writes in silence,
from between the chapters, from the places even
gods won't read.

And the next page?

It belongs to her.

End of Secret Chapter.

Chapter Two: Loki in the Between Realms (Where Plot Holes Go to Die)

There was a pop.
Then a flicker.
Then… absolutely nothing.

That's how Loki knew he was somewhere important.

He floated.

Or maybe he was standing.
Or lying sideways.
Gravity in the Between Realms had terrible manners.

"Well, this is… aggressively unhelpful," he muttered, poking at a nearby memory fragment that was playing in reverse.

It showed him and Aurelya arguing about

whether or not soup counted as a beverage.
He won that one. Technically.
The memory rewound, played again, then
blinked out like a broken gif.

Loki stepped forward.

The Between Realms was stitched together with:
  • broken promises,
  • abandoned plot threads,
  • and unused character arcs.

It smelled like burnt parchment and regret.

He passed a door labelled "Chapter 8B: Thor
Learns to Yodel" and wisely kept walking.

A shadow of a goat floated by, chewing an
invisible cloud.

"Okay. I'm definitely glitched."

But then something shifted.

A flicker.
A heartbeat.

Not his.

A memory wasn't just repeating.
It was changing.

Aurelya's voice.
But not the one he knew.

"You don't belong in her version," it whispered.
"You belonged to me."

Loki turned.

And there she stood.

Aurexia.

Hair like Starfire.
Eyes like betrayal sculpted into starlight.
Wearing a crown of scorched ink.

"You erased me," she said simply.
"Even you."

Loki swallowed.
For once, no smirk, no sarcasm.

"I didn't... I didn't know you existed."
Aurexia held out her hand.

"Then come remember."

Before he could protest,
before he could blink,
she pressed a black-glass page to his chest.

And every version of her he had ever loved and
abandoned came crashing back at once.

Loki screamed.

Then disappeared into ink.

Chapter Three: The Memory That Wasn't Supposed to Stay

Loki expected pain.

He did not expect… a kitchen.

He blinked.

There was flour on the floor.
A kettle boiling over.
A dragon sulking in the sink because it wasn't
allowed near the scones.
A lion chasing a mop like it was a sworn enemy.

And in the middle of it all, her.

Not Aurelya.

But the first version.

Aurexia.

She was radiant in her chaos.
More fire than flower.
More prophecy than poem.

She shoved a burnt tray onto the counter and
pointed at him with a wooden spoon.

"If you're going to time-walk into my kitchen, at
least stir something."

Loki didn't move. He just… stared.

Because he remembered this.
This exact moment.
And how it ended.

Back then, he hadn't said "I love you."
Back then, he'd laughed and vanished before it
got serious.

"Too messy," he'd said.
"Too real."

But now?

Now he remembered what came after.

The rejection.
The rewrite.

The way she had been folded into ash and replaced.

By Aurelya, warm, kind, lovely Aurelya.

But not her.

Suddenly, the kitchen burned away.

He stood in a hundred scenes all at once.
- Aurexia, bleeding ink in a library no one ever visited.
- Aurexia, fighting for a realm that would delete her before ever thanking her.
- Aurexia, holding a pen in one hand… and a memory of him in the other.

"You forgot me," she whispered through every version of her.
"You replaced me with a softer edit of the truth."

Loki fell to his knees in the space between scenes.

Not because he was in pain, but because the weight of remembering was too much.

"You were never supposed to be erased," he breathed.

Aurexia stepped forward.

She knelt in front of him.
Lifted his chin.

"I don't want revenge," she lied.
"I just want you to choose the truth."

And in her hand…
she offered him a pen.
Not black. Not gold.
Just… clear.

"Write your version."

"But if you lie… I'll know."

Chapter Four: The Version Loki Couldn't Tell

He stared at the pen.

It was clear like glass.
But when he held it, it felt heavy.
Like every lie he'd ever told had weight… and the ink was made of regret.

"Write," Aurexia said softly.
"I just want the truth."

Loki hated being pinned.
He hated being seen.

He hated that her voice didn't shake.
That she wasn't begging to be remembered.
That she was just… waiting.

So he took a breath.

And he wrote:

"Version 1 – The Edited Truth"
You were too much fire.

I ran.
I chose the version of you who let me stay in the spotlight,
and never burned too hot to stand beside.

Aurelya was safe.
You were not.

The pen glowed but didn't stop.

Loki's hand shook.
But he kept writing.

"Version 2 – The Real Truth"

I loved you.
But I didn't believe you'd survive the rewrite.
I didn't fight for you because I didn't want to watch you break.
I didn't choose her.
I abandoned you and they made her from the empty space I left.

He stopped.
He wanted to smirk.
To twist the moment into a joke.
But there was nothing clever about honesty.
He looked up.

And Aurexia was crying.
But not sad.

Relieved.

"Thank you," she whispered.
"That... that was the version I wanted to read."

She kissed his forehead.

"Now go back to her."

Loki blinked.

"What?"

"She's glitching, isn't she?" Aurexia smiled.
"The world's losing her, piece by piece. She
doesn't know why. But I do."

"Then help her," Loki said.

"No," Aurexia said, standing tall.
"You do it. You wrote the truth. That makes you
the bridge."

She raised her hand and erased herself.
Line by line.

Loki screamed again.
Too late.
Just like last time.

But this time…
he remembered everything.

And he knew what he had to do.

Mini Flashback Chapter:

The Flame and the Trickster

(Buried between rewritten drafts where no love story ever survived unchanged)

It wasn't a kiss.
It wasn't a prophecy.
It wasn't some dramatic Realm-saving act.

It was soup.

Loki had broken into the Temple of the 5th Draft,
hacked a sacred scroll to read "free snack coupons,"
and was hiding from Realm Guards in a half-collapsed tavern with Aurexia
who was very clearly pretending not to care.

"You're bleeding," she said, not looking at him.

"It's an artistic choice," Loki replied, trying to pretend he hadn't been stabbed by a poetic metaphor guard.

"Hold still."

She didn't heal him with magic.
She didn't whisper ancient words.
She just… tore a strip from her cloak, wrapped it around his arm, and poured him soup.

"You're not invincible," she said.

"Tell that to my ego," he grinned.

"I'm serious, Loki."

He looked up.

Her eyes weren't just starlight.

They were storm light.

"I see you," she said quietly.

"And I don't care how many versions they try to write you into… this is the one I'll remember."

That was the first time anyone had looked at Loki and not tried to fix him, tame him, or use him.

She wasn't asking for him to be good.

She just wanted him to be real.

And that's when it happened.

Loki, for once, didn't make a joke.
Didn't run.
Didn't vanish.

He just held the bowl of soup and said nothing.

Because the words that burned his tongue –
"I love you too" –
were not in the script.

And the moment passed.
And so did she.

Soon rewritten.
Erased.
Forgotten.

But not now.

Now he remembered.

End of Flashback Chapter

Secret Chapter: The Footnote

There is a library that no one catalogues.
A shelf that doesn't appear in maps of the
Realms.
A page that rewrites itself only when it's read by
the one it was meant for.

And today…
Aurelya finds it.

She's been glitching all morning.

Names flicker.
Memories fade in mid-sentence.
Her reflection doesn't always match her face.

Even the dragon, usually calm, tilts its head and
sniffs at her like she's not quite… hers.

She stumbles into the library by accident.
(But nothing in the Realms is ever truly
accidental.)

There's a book with no title.

She opens it.

The pages are blank.

Until she blinks.

And then one line appears:

"To the girl who got to live my story, don't forget it's borrowed."

She freezes.

Words form again, line by line, as if someone is writing just beneath the paper, whispering into the ink:

"I was the first version of you. Fierce. Flawed. Flame born."
"They said I was too much."
"So they wrote you instead."
"This is not your fault."
"But it is now your choice."

Aurelya grips the book tighter.
The words blur, like they're trying to leave before she's done.
"The pen is yours now. But the cost is knowing."
"If you keep writing their version, you will

vanish."
"If you write your own, the Realms will burn."

"Do you want to be remembered for being soft
enough to survive?"
"Or strong enough to change the story?"

The final line writes itself in blood-red ink:

"Remember me, and you remember yourself."
A.

The page curls at the edges.
The ink begins to smoulder.

But Aurelya doesn't let go.

"I remember," she whispers.
"And I won't forget again."

End of Secret Chapter

Chapter Five: The Moment She Forgot Her Name

The dragon was the first to notice.

It circled above Aurelya three times, then landed hard, wings splayed, head tilted, nostrils flaring.

"You smell... wrong," it said.
Not angry. Not afraid.
Just confused.

The lion stayed silent.

But it walked between her and the rest of the group, not protectively... cautiously.

Like it wasn't sure who she was protecting them from.

Aurelya blinked.

She'd just said something funny, hadn't she?
Something about Thor's chicken choir and the explosive flatulence of dwarves?
Everyone had laughed. She had laughed.

And then… the laugh didn't belong to her.

"Are you alright?" Nyric asked gently.
"You glitched."

Aurelya looked at her hand.

It was flickering.
Like old film stock stuttering between frames.

"I don't know what I'm doing here," she
whispered.

Silence.

Even the squirrel stopped stealing snacks.

"You're Aurelya," Thor said firmly.
"You're… you're our chaos-tamer. The dragon's
favourite pillow. The one Loki teases because
he's too awkward to"

"No," she cut in.
"I'm someone else's rewrite."

"And I think I'm forgetting who I was supposed
to be."
The Realms around her shuddered.

Trees bent the wrong way.
Wind whispered names that weren't hers.

And behind her eyes, a door creaked open.

She saw a firelit kitchen.
A lion chasing a mop.
Soup that wasn't quite edible.

A version of herself she'd never met but always
carried.

"Aurexia," she whispered.

The moment she spoke the name, her eyes
turned gold just for a second.

And then…

"Loki's back," the dragon rumbled.

She turned.

And there he stood.

Dishevelled.
Smeared in ink.
Breathing like he'd fought the universe and
cheated at least twice.

"You remember," she said, her voice breaking.

"I do," he replied.
"And I'm not going to forget you again. Either of you."

The sky cracked.

A line of light split the air above them
a pen stroke tearing through the narrative itself.

"Then we have to fix the story," Aurelya said.
"Before the Realms choose one of us... and erase the other forever."

Chapter Six: The Rewrite Strikes First

It started with the trees.

Not whispering.
Screaming.

The bark curled back, ink bleeding from the cracks.
Leaves dissolved midair, rewriting themselves into blank parchment as they fell.

Then came the sky.

Not thunder.
Typing.

Lines forming overhead like ancient quills gone rogue.
Letters appearing in clouds:

"CORRUPTION DETECTED. INITIATE RESTRUCTURE."

Loki grabbed Aurelya's hand.

"That's new."
"That's us," she replied, eyes glowing again.
"The Realms are trying to overwrite everything
back to before me. Before… us."

The lion growled.

The dragon flared.

Even Nyric swore in six dialects of ancient script.

The grass beneath them shifted into words.
Actual words.

"Aurelya: Reclassify as Artifact. Remove from
Timeline."

"Loki: Anomaly. Contain or erase."

"They're not just rewriting," Nyric said, pulling
open a scroll that was updating in real time.
"They're replacing your whole narrative arc.
With a new one."

A shimmer appeared in the sky, a portal lined in
red wax and editor's notes.

And from it stepped an Archivist.
Tall.

Faceless.
Ink dripping from its fingers.

It spoke in publishing deadlines and
bureaucratic cruelty.
"Please remain calm as you are deleted," it
intoned.

"This process is entirely non-negotiable and
extremely painful."

Loki drew his daggers.

"You'll have to revise me from my cold, dramatic
hands."

But Aurelya didn't move.

She was staring at the grass.

Because a single line was still being written:

"Aurexia: Unknown Entity. Access: Forbidden."

Her hand pulsed gold and red at once.

"I'm not being erased," she whispered.
"I'm being split."
And suddenly…

She was.

Aurelya fell to her knees.
Her shadow twisted, tore and began pulling itself
upright.

A second figure.
Hair darker.
Eyes sharper.

Wearing her face but not her soul.

"Oh gods," Loki breathed.
"That's not a rewrite. That's a reboot."

"RUN," the dragon shouted.

And they did.

With the Archivist behind them,
and Aurexia's form rising from a fracture in
reality
no longer forgotten…

…but re-inserted.

Chapter Seven: The Flight Through the Crumbling Realms

The map was lying.
It said the path went left through the Forest of
Misremembered Monarchs.
But left was now… gone.

Trees crumbled into timelines that didn't
happen.
Rocks rearranged into plot devices.
Even the clouds tried to narrate over them like
pushy museum guides.

"This is the worst time for a Realm-wide reboot,"
Nyric muttered, dodging a floating flashback of
his own birth.

"Define worst," Loki gasped, still dragging a
reluctant goat that had somehow gotten caught
in the chaos.

"The part where the mountain is now made of
deleted dialogue," the lion growled.

"And the part where it's chasing us," the dragon
added.

They ran.

Each Realm they crossed flickered, rebooting
into a version it had almost become:
   • In the 7th Realm, they found a utopia written
entirely by self-help bocks. They lasted 32
seconds.
   • In the Realm of the Exes, Aurelya punched a
very familiar-looking character named "L-0K3"
in the face before running again.
   • The 10th Realm tried to loop them back to
the beginning.

Only one thing kept them grounded:

Aurelya was still holding the page.
The one with Aurexia's message.
And it hadn't burned. Not yet.

Then silence.

Too quiet.

The kind of quiet that usually means a plot twist.

They stepped into a wide expanse.

Flat.
Empty.
White.

"Is this... a loading screen?" Thor whispered.

"It's worse," Loki said, stepping forward.

"It's the Editor's Desk."

From the nothingness, a voice boomed.

Not loud but final.

"This story is broken," it said.
"We will rewrite from scratch. Delete all anomalies. Beginning with… you."

Aurelya dropped the page.

It hit the ground like thunder.

And the Realms paused.

Just long enough.

"NOW!" she shouted.

Loki stabbed the air with the Pen of Intention.
Nyric threw a scroll that exploded into punctuation.
The lion roared his first full roar, shaking the void.

And the dragon ignited.

They tore open a side realm.
A crack.
A space between chapters.

And they jumped.

Behind them, the Editor screamed.

But they were already gone.

Chapter Eight: Aurexia: First of Her Name, Last of Their Mistakes

She opened her eyes in silence.

No fanfare.
No prophecy.
No applause.

Just a blinking cursor in the sky.

"Welcome back, anomaly."

She stood.

No longer flickering.
No longer fading.

She was real now but not just real.

She was written.
Intentionally.
Finally.

And before her, floating like a god's discarded to-do list, hovered the System Console of the Editor.

She smiled.

"Oh, look. They left it unlocked."

Flick.
Swipe.
Rewrite.

Reality bent beneath her fingers.

She rewrote her scars into stars.
Her absence into authority.
Her exile into access.

"Let's see," she whispered, scrolling through narrative files.
"Version 3.7 Aurelya… too soft."
"Version 4.2 Loki… still a coward."
"Dragon: loyal. Keep."
"Lion: rename pending."

Then she found it:

THE DELETE REQUEST.

Filed by: THE COLLECTIVE NARRATORS
Status: Approved
Target: AUREXIA
Reason: "Too much fire. Too little obedience."

She didn't scream.
She just highlighted it.
And rewrote the reason.

"Reason for deletion:
Scared of what she could become."

She hit [ENTER].
And the page caught fire, not to destroy…

But to resurrect.
"You wanted a softer version," she whispered.
"You got it. But now you'll remember the price."

Her hair flared red.
Her eyes gold.
The ink in her veins glowed.
And in her hand appeared a new pen.
Its name etched in a language only villains speak
fluently:

"The Editor's Quill."

She turned to the blank realm behind her.

And wrote a single command:

"Let them run. Let them hope. But I will write the final line."

Chapter Nine: Welcome to the Realm of Unfinished Stories

The landing was undramatic.

No explosions.
No magic sparks.

Just a slow splat into a very confused paragraph about pirate ballerinas and sentient toast.

"Where the Hel are we?" Thor muttered, peeling a slice of emotionally fragile bread off his boot.

"Either a cursed idea board," said Nyric, "or the Realm of Unfinished Stories."

"Wait," said Aurelya. "Is that"

She pointed.

A minotaur in a tutu was crying into a plotline that just read:
'AND THEN SOMETHING AWESOME HAPPENS.'

The sky was made of chapter outlines.
The ground was thick with rejected titles.
There was a breeze that whispered half-finished metaphors like:

"Her soul was like a… like a… um… never mind."

The gang looked around.

A three-headed llama sobbed in the distance.
A romance subplot sat alone at a bar, unfinished, weeping into a mojito.

And in the middle of it all was a glowing, flickering Book Tree its branches full of chapters that had never been claimed.

"This place is unstable,' Loki said, staring at a bush that kept turning into side characters.
"It's where all forgotten stories go," Aurelya whispered.
"Ones the Realms rejected."

The dragon snorted.
"So basically, this is the landfill of narrative potential."

Suddenly, the lion perked up.

Then growled.

"Someone's here," it said.

The ground rumbled.

Pages fluttered.

And from the shadows stepped

"Hi," said a small girl. "Are you here to finish me?"

She couldn't have been more than ten.

Wearing a cloak made of manuscript paper. Eyes glowing with unreleased plot twists.

"I'm Chapter 0," she said.
"No one ever wrote me. So, I started writing myself."

She held up a glowing inkpot.

"But I don't know how to end. And now the unfinished stories are waking up."
Behind her, something stirred.
A giant, malformed villain concept missing most of its personality crawled from a plot hole.

A dozen half-built sidekicks swarmed behind it,
all of them broken, forgotten, unstable.

"If we don't help her," Aurelya said,
"this Realm won't just collapse…"

"It'll try to merge with ours."

Chapter Ten: Into the Book Tree

The Book Tree loomed above them.

Its bark pulsed with forgotten lines.
Its branches whispered with abandoned dialogue.
Its roots curled around sealed chapters, each labelled with names no one had spoken aloud in a very long time.

"This place feels like déjà vu wrapped in anxiety," Loki muttered, brushing inkdust off his cloak.

"It's worse," said Chapter 0, leading the way. "This is where your story stopped."

As they stepped into the hollow trunk, glowing scrolls flickered to life on the walls, not with light, but with memory.

Each scroll snapped toward its owner like a wand choosing a wizard.
- Nyric's scroll hissed and showed a

father he never named.

• The lion's scroll just read: "ROAR: Not Yet Claimed."

• The dragon refused to take theirs at all. ("Mine's in another genre," they said.)

• Thor's scroll played a slideshow of goats in Armor, intercut with a missing moment where he'd almost quit being a god.

And then Aurelya touched hers.

It glowed red and gold.

Her scroll unrolled violently, pages flipping themselves, revealing a chapter that had been blacked out.

Only one word shone through:

"Aurexia."

"This is the piece they removed from me," she whispered.

"This is the piece I need to finish… or I'll never be whole again."
Loki touched his scroll
and gasped.

It showed a scene not yet written:
Him, on his knees.
Aurexia's hand outstretched.
And the words "CHOOSE" echoing over and over again.

"I'm supposed to choose between them," he said quietly.

"Between who I loved… and who I never let myself love."

Chapter 0 climbed onto a branch and pointed deeper into the glowing library.

"The answers you need are in there," she said.

"But so are the ghosts of your unspoken endings. And they bite."

The gang stared into the shadows of their own unwritten truths.

And stepped forward.

One scroll at a time.
End of Chapter Ten

Chapter Eleven: The Split That Was Always There

The scroll shimmered like glass over boiling water.
One moment it showed Aurelya laughing, alive, fingers smudged with ink.

The next Aurexia a fire-eyed goddess rewriting the Realms with a quill sharp enough to cut fate in half.

"Loki," Chapter 0 said softly.
"It's choosing for you. Or maybe… showing you who you already chose."

"No," he whispered.
"It's doing what the Realms never let me do."

"It's letting me finish both."

The scroll split.

So did he.

One version fell left
into the timeline of Aurelya.
Warm. Chaotic. Funny. Herself.

One version fell right
into the rewrite.
Where Aurexia waited in silence, her smile sharp
enough to sever history.

LEFT TIMELINE WITH AURELYA

They're sitting on a floating dock of memory
fragments.
She's trying to braid the dragon's tail. It's not
going well.

"You always come back," she says.

"Only when it's you," he replies.

"What happens if I'm not?"

"Then I'll stay lost."
RIGHT TIMELINE WITH AUREXIA

They're in the Editor's chamber.
Aurexia stands beside a burning manuscript.

"This world rejected me," she says.
"But you never did."

"You were the first thing that made sense," he replies.
"Before sense was allowed."

"If you stay," she says, voice low, "we win."

"If I stay," he breathes, "I lose her."

LEFT TIMELINE

The dock crumbles.
Aurelya shouts.
Loki grabs her hand.

"I'm slipping," she says

"Then I'll fall with you," he replies.

But something pulls him.

RIGHT TIMELINE

Aurexia offers the Editor's Quill.

"Write your name beside mine."

"And if I do?" he asks.

"You'll never hurt again."

REAL WORLD OUTSIDE BOTH TIMELINES

The scroll cracks in midair.

Both versions of Loki collide.
Reality screams.

And one version drops to his knees, gasping,
bleeding ink whispering:

"She… chose for me."

Behind him, the scroll reseals.

A single sentence left glowing:

"The story only has one ending, but the heart
remembers every chapter."

He stands.

Looks up.

And only one name is on his lips

Chapter Twelve: The Chapter They Burned

The scroll unrolled like a wound.

Blank.

Then bleeding.

Then full of words she didn't write but somehow remembered.

"Chapter 21: Aurelya Before She Was Edited."

It began slowly.

A girl.

Not glowing.

Not chosen.

Just fighting to be heard in a world too loud to listen.

She saw herself

not as the Celestial

not as the Chosen

but as the scrapheap version

of someone they thought they could improve.

She wasn't funny.

She was angry.

She wasn't soft.

She was jagged.

She didn't inspire the Realms.

She dared them to admit they were broken.

"You were a threat," the scroll wrote, in her own voice.

"So, they rewrote you into something safe."

The dragon peered over her shoulder.

"Is that you?"

"It was."

"Do you want her back?"

"I don't know."

"She's still in there," said the lion gently.

"Roaring quieter. But still roaring."

Then the scroll glitched and the ink screamed.

Aurexia's handwriting appeared bold, defiant:

"YOU WERE MEANT TO BE ME."

"STOP LIVING AS THEIR COMPROMISE."

Aurelya staggered back, clutching her head.

Memories not hers poured in.

- A first kiss with Loki that never happened.

- A conversation with Odin where she won the argument.

- A war she started and won.

- A life she was supposed to have.

"They gave me a quieter fate," she whispered.

"And now she wants it back."

The scroll burned but didn't disintegrate.

Instead, it folded into a single page and embedded itself in her palm.

Like a weapon.

Or a curse.

Or a key.

“We're not ready for her,” Nyric said quietly.

“No,” Aurelya said. “But she's already coming.”

Chapter Thirteen: The Loki That Came Back

The air shimmered like a nervous thought.

The Book Tree groaned its branches bowing under the weight of a returning soul.

And then…

he was there.

Loki stumbled out of a fracture in the scroll.

Half-wrapped in static.
Eyes darker than before.

Not evil.
Not broken.

Just…

older.

"It's you," Aurelya breathed.

"Is it?" he asked.

"You tell me."

She stepped forward, slow.

"What's the last thing you remember?"

He closed his eyes.

"Two timelines. One heartbeat."
"She let me go."
"You pulled me back."

Her hands trembled.

"Then it's really you."

"It is," he whispered.
"But not exactly."

He held up the Editor's Quill.

It was cracked burned at the tip.

"I had to break it… from the inside."

"That means Aurexia?"

"Still rising," he said.
"But now she knows I chose you."

The lion sniffed him.

Snorted.

"He's not lying."

The dragon stared long.

Then curled its tail protectively around them both.

"We don't have time for guilt.
We have time for war."

Aurelya looked at him again.
Really looked.

He still wore mischief like a second skin.
Still smiled with secrets.
But now…

He was shaking.

"Loki," she said gently.
"What did you have to give up to make it back?"

He looked at her.

And for once, didn't deflect with a joke.

"A version of myself that loved her too."

"But I remembered this:
You saw the real me first.
You laughed when I deserved scolding.
You stayed when I made it impossible."

He stepped closer.

Held out the shattered quill.

"I don't know how to win this war."

"But I know who I want beside me when it ends."

And she took it.

The quill.
His hand.
The weight of his choice.

Not as a prize.
But as a promise.

Chapter Fourteen: The War Begins

The Book Tree howled.

Not in fear

but in warning.

Pages ripped themselves free.

Ink bled down bark.

And every scroll that had once been forgotten now opened its eyes…

Because the rewritten had come to fight.

The first tear in the sky was silent.

Just a seam of gold light, like a paper cut across the clouds.

Then came the noise

A sound like every scream ever edited out of history

shouting itself back into existence.

"They're here," whispered Chapter 0, clutching a page shield.

"Aurexia's army. The rewritten."

From the breach poured them:

• Heroes with forced redemption arcs all smiles, no souls.

• Villains stripped of complexity, turned into hollow clichés.

• Side characters promoted to power not because they earned it, but because the rewrite demanded it.

And leading them was a general made of pure plot armour.

Literally.

Shining. Unstoppable.

Immune to critique.

"That's 'Sir Narrative Justification,'" Loki groaned.

"I hate that guy."

Aurelya raised the Editor's cracked quill like a dagger.

"Everyone take position!" she shouted.

"We're defending the stories that never got a chance."

The battle broke instantly.

• Thor rode in on his line-dancing chickens, each now wearing shimmering hen-mail forged by the elves.

• Nyric lobbed sarcasm-laced scrolls like grenades, they exploded with unresolved character trauma.

• The lion finally roared, cracking through three villains and a flashback.

And the dragon?

The dragon set fire to every "chosen one" with no actual growth arc.

Then a thunderclap:

Aurexia stepped through the breach.

Cloaked in every page the Realms had tried to hide.

"You can't stop the rewrite," she called, voice booming.

"I'm not the villain. I'm the version they didn't want you to see."

Aurelya stepped forward.

Quill in one hand. Scroll-shield in the other.

"Then let's show them the version they didn't expect."

They charged.

Sister against sister.

Ink against ink.

The story against itself.

Chapter Fifteen: Loki and the Realm That Was Never Named

He didn't tell the others.

He just winked at the lion.

Dropped a half-written goodbye on the dock.

And vanished.

"Where are we going?" asked the squirrel, riding in his hood again.

"Someplace older than endings," Loki replied.

"Where ideas go before, they're born."

He stepped off the map.

Literally.

The edges curled as he passed.

Ink peeled backward.

Even his name flickered.

WELCOME TO THE REALM THAT WAS NEVER NAMED.

The sign wrote itself in midair.

Then fell apart.

This place… didn't exist.

Not officially.

But here were things:

• A bridge made of metaphors no one understood.

• A tree that grew character flaws instead of fruit.

• A lake filled with titles that never found their stories.

And in the centre

an ancient desk.

Dusty. Cracked.

Still holding a pen.

He approached.

"Hello?" Loki said.

"I'm looking for the Author."

No response.

Only the wind

turning a single page

of an unfinished book

that had his name on it.

"You shouldn't be here," said a voice.

Loki turned.

A man stepped forward.

Wearing no face.

Wearing every face.

Part Reader. Part Writer.

"Are you the Author?"

"Sometimes," the figure replied.

"When the story lets me."

"Then write me a way to fix this," Loki demanded.

"Aurexia, the Realms, the rewrite fix it."

The Author stared at him.

"I can't."

"You made the story!"

"I started it," the Author said.

"But you made it matter "

The Author pointed to the pen on the desk.

"You want to fix the Realms?"

"Write the one thing no narrator can fake."

"What's that?"

"Truth."

Loki picked up the pen.

It was warm.

Alive.

Like it remembered how he used to lie.

He opened the book with his name on it.

"Then let's start with this," he whispered.

And he wrote:

"I was never the villain.

But I liked being mistaken for one."

The page glowed.

And the wind stopped.

Behind him, a door appeared

back to the battlefield.

But this time, with something different in his heart:

Not a trick.

Not a riddle.

But a truth he chose to carry.

Chapter Sixteen: The Trickster Carries the Truth

The sky was still tearing when he returned.

Chickens fled in armour.
The Book Tree bled metaphors.
Thor was arguing with a rewritten bard over
whether "YOLO" belonged in battle poetry.

And then

A rupture.
A ripple.
A return.

Loki stepped through the page.

Unscarred.
Unhurried.
Holding a single sentence in glowing script.
"You left," Aurelya said, voice tight with worry.

"I went to find the first truth," he replied.
"And it nearly unmade me."
He handed her the page.
It was written in his handwriting.

But not the usual flourishes.
This was simpler.
Older.
Real.

"I have lied to survive.
But I told her the truth and still lost.
So now I'll speak truth. . even if it breaks me."

Aurelya stared at it.

Then stared at him.

"She'll hate you for it."
"She already does," Loki said.
"But that's because she still hopes I'll lie again."

Thunder cracked.

From across the battlefield, Aurexia turned.
She saw the page.

She saw him.
And she screamed.

"THAT TRUTH WAS NEVER YOURS TO TELL!"

"Then why are you so afraid of it?" he shouted
back.
The battlefield froze.

Even the rewritten characters paused.
Even the sky held its breath.

Because the one thing the Realms couldn't
rewrite…

Was what he'd brought back.

"This page is from the Author," Loki said, lifting it
high.

"And it proves the one thing you buried"

"Aurelya and Aurexia were never split to weaken
them."

"They were split… because together, they could
end you."

Aurexia recoiled.
But not in pain.
In recognition.

She remembered.
The final lock on the Realms snapped.

Not from a sword.
Not from a quill.

But from the truth spoken aloud:

"You weren't erased because you were wrong,"
Loki said.
"You were erased because you were right too
soon."

Aurexia stepped back.

The rewritten behind her began to glitch.
One by one… they remembered themselves.

And Loki?

He didn't grin.

He didn't bow.

He just stood beside Aurelya

finally honest.

Chapter Seventeen: The Fracture Before the Finale

The Book Tree moaned like a breaking spine.

Then
a crack louder than thunder,
brighter than prophecy,
and deeper than plot.

The sky didn't split.

It folded.

"No no, no, this wasn't supposed to happen!" cried Chapter 0.

"What's happening?" Aurelya shouted.

"The Realms aren't just collapsing they're detaching."

"From what?!"

"From each other. From logic. From genre."
BOOM.

The battlefield warped like melted ink.
One by one, the heroes fell

into unfinished books.
Abandoned drafts.
Lost stories with no endings.

Thor was swallowed by a cookbook from the
Age of Giants.

He landed in a flour avalanche, armed with
chickens and no idea how to bake.

Nyric crash-landed into a children's fable where
lying made your nose grow

Which was a problem, because sarcasm counted.

The dragon ended up in a love story set in
space.

The lion got pulled into an emo vampire
detective series with a tragic backstory and an
even more tragic hat.

And Aurelya?
She vanished into a book that had no title.

Just a page with the words:

"The Hero Who Refused the Ending."

"Where's Loki?!" Aurelya shouted into the void.

No answer.

Only a page drifting by:

"To find the last answer, the Trickster must face the first question."

And Aurexia?

She didn't fall.

She jumped.

Straight into the most dangerous story ever written:

"The Draft The Author Was Afraid To Finish."

Now, the Realms don't just need saving.
They need rewriting.
And Book Five?

Closes not with a resolution…

...but with a table of contents rearranged by fate.

End of Book Five: The War of the Unwritten

BOOK SIX

THE LIBRARY
THAT EATS
ENDINGS

Chapter One: Loki and the Desk of Terrible Decisions

Loki landed face-first in a pile of self-help scrolls.

"You are the plot twist you've been waiting for," one whispered.

"Oh gods," Loki groaned. "I've fallen into the Motivational Section."

The lights flickered.
A sign above him flashed:

WELCOME, UNFINISHED CHAOS.
"Please do not eat the books."
"Or drink with them."

"Squirrel?" Loki called.

"Here."
The squirrel emerged from a romance novel wearing a tiny feather boa and dragging a rejection letter.
"It was getting steamy."
"Put it back," Loki said. "That's not canon."

He crept through the shelves.

Some whispered his old names:
God of Mischief. Liar of Nine Realms. Guy Who
Ruined That One Dinner Party.

Others just said:

"You again."

"Thought you were deleted."

"We don't do refunds."

Then he saw it.

A desk in the distance.
Ancient. Ominous.
Stacked with pages… and a sign that said:
DO NOT TOUCH.
(Especially you, Loki.)

"Well now I have to."
He touched it.
Naturally, it exploded.

Ink shot everywhere.
Plot holes flew like ninja stars.
A drawer opened and screamed,

"WE WARNED YOU!"

And then…

A single envelope floated down.

Black wax. Gold seal. One word:

"Trickster."

Loki opened it.

Inside:
A map.
A punchline.
And a note:

"You want to fix this story?"
"You'll need a team.
The worst-written heroes from every genre
ever."

"Oh no," Loki said.

"Oh yes," whispered the desk.

Chapter Two: Aurelya and the Romance Trope Apocalypse

Aurelya landed in a velvet chaise lounge.

Which was weird, since the last thing she remembered was being swallowed by a book with no title.

She sat up slowly.

The room was dimly lit, draped in rose petals, violins playing somewhere in the walls. Everything smelled faintly of heartbreak and cinnamon.

"Oh no," she muttered.
"I'm in a romance arc."

Footsteps echoed dramatically.

A brooding stranger approached shirt unbuttoned just enough to be legally obligated in this genre.

"Have we met before?" he whispered.
"Because my soul just remembered yours."

Aurelya blinked.
Then punched him.

He vanished in a puff of glitter.

A spotlight flared.

From the shadows:
• A cowboy poet with a tragic past.
• A CEO who needed to be shown how to love.
• A vampire with great hair and bad boundaries.

They circled her like plotlines with nowhere else
to go.

"I don't have time for your redemption arcs!" she
shouted, conjuring the scroll embedded in her
palm.

The air sizzled.

The scroll glowed.

And a doorway opened leading into the next aisle
of the library:

Genre: Paranormal Thriller with Unresolved
Trauma.

The cowboy poet tipped his hat.
"You'll be back. They always come back."

Aurelya flipped him off politely and stepped through the door.

Behind her, the Romance Trope Apocalypse wept into a torn love letter and softly played "My Heart Will Go On."

Chapter Three: Loki Assembles the Plot-Holes

"You can't fix the Realms with heart," said the letter.
"You need backstory damage, questionable dialogue, and just enough fanfiction energy to cause a small fire."

"So… me," Loki grinned.

He turned the map.

The quest:
Collect the worst-written characters the Library ever locked away.
Because sometimes, it takes a disaster to stop an apocalypse.
 First recruit: Brooding Vampire Bard™

Loki found him in the Gothic Wing, standing in front of a broken mirror and whispering:

"My soul is an echo that only weeps in minor keys."
"I'm sorry, are you reciting poetry to your own

reflection?" Loki asked.
"Yes. And he's not responding."

"Perfect. You're hired."

Next: Sexy Amnesiac Ninja™

Found in the Action-Romance-Cringe crossover aisle, mid-fight with her own dramatic flashbacks.

"Who am I?" she whispered, high-kicking a bookshelf.

"Doesn't matter," Loki said.
"You're mysterious, dangerous, and your outfit defies physics. On the team."

"Wait do I know you?"

"No, but I'm 90% sure we had a thing in Book Four."

 Finally: The Talking Cactus Who Thinks He's a Wizard

"BEHOLD," the cactus bellowed, toppling off a shelf.
"I AM THORNUS THE ENCHANTED. GUARDIAN

OF THE LOST DUST JACKET."

"...You're a succulent in a top hat."
"A MAGE, you uncultured zucchini!"
"You're in."

Loki stepped back, admiring his misfit team:
   • A depressed undead musician with eyeliner for days
   • A ninja with zero memory and at least five unresolved love triangles
   • And a plant with delusions of wizardry and access to exploding glitter spells

"We're gonna die," whispered the squirrel.

"Oh no," Loki smirked.
"We're going to win poorly."

Chapter Four: Mirror Aurelya

The Mirror Pages didn't shimmer.
They pulsed.
Like they were breathing.

Aurelya stepped forward, hand hovering over
the reflection that wasn't quite her own.

Her lion growled low.
Her dragon stayed silent.
Even the squirrel somehow back from Loki's
chaos refused to look.

Because this wasn't just a mirror.
It was a chapter still being written.

And inside?

She was already there.

Mirror Aurelya stood with perfect posture.
Her wings were polished.
Her crown? Straight.
Not a single hair out of place.
"You found me," the reflection said.
"You're… me?" Aurelya asked.

"No," the reflection replied. "I'm what you could have been."

The Room Split.
• On the left: Sacrifice.
Every choice Mirror Aurelya made, she made for others.
She never laughed at Loki's jokes.
Never let her dragon eat an entire banquet table for fun.
She was respected.

And so alone.

• On the right: Rebellion.
Aurelya's real path.
The one with bad puns, unspoken grief, and way too many detours through chaos.
The one where she chose love over prophecy.
Loki over legend.

"I traded peace for obedience," said Mirror Aurelya.
"You traded power for jcy."
"And do you regret it?" Aurelya asked
"I... don't know anymore."

They reached for each other.

And the page flipped.

The mirror shattered silently.
Their fingers touched.
And just like that

They were on the other side.

Aurelya blinked.

She was wearing… ceremonial robes?
People were bowing?
Someone handed her a diplomatic scroll and a
list of war treaties?

"Wait. NO. NOPE. I DON'T DO BUREAUCRACY"

Meanwhile…

Mirror Aurelya looked down at a dragon
chewing on a roast duck and a lion tangled in
ribbon.
"…I think I'm going to like it here."

End of Chapter Four

Chapter Five: The Vault of Forbidden Genres

The Vault loomed before them.

Six stories high.
Twelve locks.
Guarded by a floating thesaurus that judged your vocabulary in real time.

A sign above the massive doors read:

GENRES TOO misplaced modifiers.

They hissed every time someone used passive voice.

"She was walking"
HISS HISS HISS

"I WALKED, okay?!" screamed the cactus.
"Sweet cactus Christ, fine."

One gremlin exploded in joy and threw a semicolon.

Obstacle #2: The Sentient Thesaurus
It floated into their path, glowing and dramatic.

"State your purpose," it boomed.

"We seek the Truth of the Forbidden Genres,"
Loki said.

"Define 'truth' using three synonyms and a
haiku."

"…"

"Or," Loki whispered, "we could distract it."

"How?"

"With him." [Points to the Bard.]

The Bard stepped forward, smouldering, and
recited:

"Thy loquacious lexicon lingers like longing in
labyrinths of"

"YES," the Thesaurus gasped. "YOU GET ME."

While they bonded over esoteric verbiage, Loki
picked the lock with a stolen subplot and a bit of

ninja wire.
Inside the Vault
Dust.
Silence.
And then:

BOOM.

A gust of glitter and the roar of a long-buried genre.

Books flew by:
 • "Alien Cowboys of Emotional Reckoning"
 • "Underwater Courtroom Drama: A Merman's Justice"
 • "Choose-Your-Own-Midlife Crisis: The Gamebook"

And one glowing tome in the back:
"The Last Rewrite."

"This is it," Loki whispered.

"The genre that was too unstable to contain."

"The one the Author abandoned because it could undo everything."

"And we're going to steal it."

The cactus raised a tiny glitter wand.

"FOR CHAOS, PURPOSE, AND GLORIOUS NARRATIVE ANARCHY!"

"...And snacks," the ninja added. STRANGE, STUPID, OR SENTIENT TO PUBLISH.
No entry without plot armour.

"This is madness," the Bard whispered.

"No," Loki grinned.
"This... is narrative liberation."

"Still sounds like madness."

"Same genre, different font."

Obstacle #1: The Grammar Gremlins

Tiny creatures with red pens, berets, and a rage for

Chapter Six: Mirror Aurelya Joins the Plot

Mirror Aurelya had been in the Realms exactly three days
…and she was done with the lack of structure.

The dragon refused to land on time.
The lion had no scheduled naps.
And the squirrel?
Kept ordering enchanted delivery food and tipping in riddles.

"This isn't a rebellion," she muttered.
"This is an unmonitored creative retreat disguised as an existential crisis."

She found Loki's team purely by accident.
(Translation: she followed the trail of glitter, bad metaphors, and dramatic sighing.)

And what she saw?
  • A vampire rehearsing his tragic monologue to a wall.
  • A ninja using her own backstory as a skipping rope.

• A cactus teaching pigeons telepathy.
"WHAT IS THIS?"

Loki turned. "Oh no. You found us."

"You're running an unauthorised genre raid without an efficiency framework?!"

"I didn't realise 'spreadsheets' was a weapon category."

Five Minutes Later

She had:
  • Named the team: The Misfit Narratives Coalition
  • Assigned roles with pie charts
  • Cross-referenced all side quests with moral alignment tables
  • And created a mission statement

"We exist to reclaim narrative agency, dismantle unjust tropes, and minimize emotional whiplash."

"You know," the cactus whispered, "I feel… organized. Like my trauma has columns now."
Loki blinked. "Okay. You can stay."

"I didn't ask for permission. I filed a Form 6B."

"What's that?"

"Request to rewrite reality."

"...Hot."

Chapter Seven: Spoiler Alert: The Ride of Ruin

It began with a quiet rumble.

Then a louder one.

Then the cactus shouting:

"I TOLD YOU NEVER TO READ THAT CHAPTER BACKWARDS!"

The Vault of Forbidden Genres was unravelling itself literally.
Paragraphs folded into staircases.
Sentences shattered into falling letters.
An entire aisle labelled "Political Erotica in Space" collapsed in on itself with a moan.

"We need an exit," Mirror Aurelya said, flipping through her Emergency Exit Plan Binder™.

"We have one," Loki said.

"You… do?"
He pointed upward.

A giant winged creature was bursting through the ceiling.
It shimmered with glowing text.
Words scrolled along its sides like leaked movie scripts.

THE SPOILER WYRM.

"It's made of cancelled trilogies and rage posts from angry fans," Loki said with reverence.
"It knows every ending.
Even the ones that haven't been written."

The Bard screamed.
The cactus saluted.
The ninja tried to fight it until her flashback distracted her mid-punch.

"He said he'd come back for me wait what?"

Mounting the Beast

The Spoiler Wyrm spoke in booming spoiler-language:

"SNAPE"
"DIES."
"BRUCE WILLIS WAS DEAD."

"DARTH VADER IS HIS DAD."
"THE CACTUS IS A PRINCE."

"I KNEW IT!" yelled the cactus, crying glitter.

They climbed on.

"Where will it take us?" Mirror Aurelya asked.

Loki just smirked.
"Where the spoilers started."

And with a roar of untold endings

They flew.

As the Vault collapsed beneath them in a glorious
disaster of genres and glitter,

the wyrm screamed its final warning:

"THE FINAL AUTHOR
ISN'T WHO YOU THINK
SHE IS"
CRASH CUT TO BLACK.

Chapter Eight: The Secret in the Silence

It was too quiet.

No dragon snoring.
No lion chewing on cushions.
Not even a squirrel scampering across forbidden
furniture with stolen snacks.

Just silence.
And efficiency.

Aurelya wandered the halls of Mirror Aurelya's
citadel.

Everything was… polished.
Perfect.
Empty.

Even her throne was cold.

On the wall hung the Prophecy Mirror, cracked at
the edges, but still alive.
It flickered with images that never were:

- A child never born.
- A realm never claimed.
- A god never loved.

Aurelya reached out
and the mirror responded.

"You weren't supposed to see this."

"Show me anyway."

The glass shimmered.
And opened.

The Secret Chapter: Page 0

She saw Mirror Aurelya younger, gentler, full of laughter.

Walking beside… Loki.
Not as friends. Not as chaos and calm.

As partners.
They danced in firelight.
Spoke of dreams.
Drew stars on each other's arms.

And then

The Author intervened.

A pen scratched across the sky.
The stars were redacted.
Their story was… deleted.

"This version of you chose duty," said the mirror.
"But only because someone rewrote her joy."

Aurelya stumbled back, breath shaking.

This wasn't about choice.
This was about control.

And now she knew:

The Author didn't just erase chapters.
She erased love.

The door behind her creaked.
A shadow stepped through.
Not the Author.
Not a villain.
Mirror Aurelya, back from her journey,
covered in ribbon and cookie crumbs.

"You saw it?" she asked quietly.

"I lived it."

"Then you understand. Why I left. Why I had to try your life."

"I do."

They looked at each other.

One with knowledge.
One with scars.

And maybe now…
a shared beginning.

Chapter Nine: Welcome to Retcon City™

"PLEASE REMEMBER TO DECLARE ALL CHARACTER GROWTH UPON ARRIVAL."
Airport-style voice as the team crash-lands in a neon-lit narrative spiral.

Retcon City wasn't just broken.
It was thriving.
- Plot holes patched with duct tape.
- NPCs selling "Trauma Paks™" on street corners.
- Characters lining up to have their worst moments erased (for a price).

Loki stared around with quiet horror.

"This place… rewrites you while you sleep."

"Then let's not nap," said the ninja, balancing on a lamppost.

"Wait," said the cactus, staring at a billboard.
"WANTED: Thornus the Unwritten.
Reward: One Canon Appearance."

"I KNEW I WAS IMPORTANT."

Plot Armour is Currency

Mirror Aurelya tried to buy a map.

"That'll be three major traumas and a season arc," said the vendor.

"All I've got is mild emotional repression and an awkward holiday episode," she replied.

"Then good luck with the alleyways."

Meanwhile…

The Bard wandered off and accidentally sold his only meaningful backstory for a song deal.

The ninja met four alternate versions of herself.
One of them was a cowboy.
Two were French.

The squirrel was elected mayor in under 11 minutes.

Loki muttered, "We need to find the Archives."

"Why?" asked Mirror Aurelya.

"Because that's where they store deleted scenes"
"and maybe… the truth behind why we were edited."

But the deeper they went, the more the city
noticed them.

Signs flickered.
Street names changed.
Billboards started listing their personal regrets.

"I don't like this," the lion growled.

"That makes two of us," said Aurelya.

"Try being hunted by your own original
character description," Loki added, ducking
behind a vending machine full of cliché weapons.

And then the screens went black.

One message appeared across the skyline:

"YOU DO NOT BELONG HERE."
"RETURN TO YOUR INTENDED ENDINGS."

But it was too late.

The ground cracked open
and a figure stepped out of a glitch in the street.

Not the Author.

Not yet.

Just someone rewritten one too many times.

"I remember you," it whispered.
"You left me on Page 17."

Chapter Ten: The Memory Loki Wouldn't Touch

It started with a whisper.
Not from the lion.
Not from the dragon.
Not from the squirrel (currently running for re-election as Mayor of Retcon).

But from the twin Aurelyas.

"Loki," they said together, cornering him in an alley between Suspicious Alleyway™ and Plot Convenience Blvd.
"It's time."
"Time for what?" he said, too casually.

"The memory. The one you locked away."

Loki tried to laugh.
But even he could feel it that ripple in the script.
The way the words were waiting.

He looked at them both.
Two versions of the same woman.
One who knew him as a myth.

One who almost knew him as home.

"If I show you this… things might not be funny
anymore."

"Then show us anyway."

The Memory Vault

Loki reached into his coat beneath the sarcasm,
behind the grief
and pulled out a crumpled, glowing scroll.
The one he never opened.
The one sealed with a feather, a flame, and a tear.

"This was supposed to be…
our ending."
He unrolled it.

And they saw:

Memory: The Day the Realms Fractured

Aurelya.
Standing at the edge of a battlefield.
Bleeding.
Brilliant.
Alone.

Loki was there
but only as a shadow in the narrative.

He wasn't written in.
He wasn't allowed.

So he broke the rules.
Stepped off the page.
And whispered something to the Author that
changed everything.

"If I can't save her in that ending…
Let me rewrite her a thousand others."

And the Author said:

"Fine. But you will forget."

Back in the present…

"That's why I joke," Loki said quietly.
"Because somewhere deep down, I knew if I
remembered this…
I'd never stop trying to rewrite it."

The twins stood in stunned silence.

The dragon curled around him.

The lion pressed close.

"You didn't just hide the truth," said Mirror
Aurelya.
"You buried yourself in it."

"I know," Loki said.

"Then dig us both out."

Chapter Eleven: Enter the Archives of Erasure

Aurelya stood before the door.

No key.
No lock.
Just an ancient carving:

"Only the forgotten may enter."

"Well," Loki muttered, "I've forgotten more versions of myself than I care to count."
"You'll be fine," the cactus said.
"I forgot my origin three books ago, and I'm thriving."

They stepped through.

And the world shifted.

The Archives

It wasn't a library.
It was a graveyard.
- Shelves of nearlys.
- Cabinets full of rewrites.
- Drawers marked "Too Emotional," "Too Soft," "Too Queer," "Too Real."

Each file glowing faintly.
Each one… humming.

The moment the twins walked in, the lights flickered.
Not from power loss.

From recognition.

"Aurelya of the First Draft," a voice called.

She turned.

And there she was.

Her.
From Chapter Zero.
The version that never made it to print.
- Wild hair.
- Fire-laced wings.

• Eyes that hadn't yet learned how to hide grief with humour.

"You left me," she said softly.
"You got edited into something readable. I got left behind."

"I didn't know"

"But he did."
She pointed behind her.

Loki.
Frozen.

Facing another Loki.

One with no smirk.
No mask.

Only rage.
And regret.
 The Confrontation

Deleted Loki stepped forward.
"You were supposed to burn it all down."

"I'm trying," current Loki said.

"No, you're dancing around the fire and calling it comedy."

The air rippled.

The scrolls began to unroll themselves.

Pages.
Tears.
Lives unlived.

The ninja found her childhood.
The cactus found a romance arc.
The Bard found out he… wasn't meant to die in Book One.

And Aurelya?
She found the first draft of her fate.
"They wanted me quiet.
They made me gentle.
But I was never that.
I was thunder in lace."

The deleted selves moved closer.

Not with vengeance.
But with purpose.

"Take us with you," they said.
"Remember us.
Write us back in."

"But won't that break the Realms?" Aurelya
asked.

Loki touched her hand.

"Maybe the Realms need to be broken…
before they can be real."

Chapter Twelve: The First Contract

They followed the scrolls.
Past the Archives.
Deeper than deletion.

To a room that shouldn't exist.

There were no books here.
Only one table.
One chair.
One parchment.

Glowing faintly.

The Contract of Creation

"What is this?" the Bard whispered.

"It's the Author's first draft," Mirror Aurelya said,
hands trembling.
"The agreement that bound the Realms
together."

It was written in ink that shimmered with

stardust.
Signed in feather, fire, and blood.
Aurelya stepped closer.
And read the words aloud:

"This world shall be governed by narrative law
where conflict shapes growth, and endings shall
reflect what is earned."

That part was known.
But below it…

A line written upside-down.
Invisible unless spoken aloud.

"And should one being remember all their lives
at once…
they may unwrite the ending
and become the pen."

Silence.

Even the dragon stopped breathing.
The squirrel fainted. Dramatically.

"So if someone remembers every version of
themselves," Loki said slowly,
"they don't just escape the story…
they become the Author."

Aurelya looked at the deleted selves behind
them.
Then at the lion.
The dragon.
At Mirror Aurelya.
At Loki.

"What if it's not just me?" she said.

"What if we all remember?"

The contract began to react.

Lines blinked.
New words started writing themselves across
the page.

And then

A single warning burned into the table:

"Only one may hold the pen."

The room shook.
The contract screamed.

And somewhere far away,
deep in a realm no longer bound by plot,
The Real Author opened her eyes.

"Someone found it," she whispered.

"Time to write them out."

Chapter Thirteen: The Betrayal of Page-Seventeen

The Archives groaned behind them.
Reality shimmered like wet ink.

Aurelya clutched the contract.
The others watched, half in awe, half in fear.

"What happens now?" the Bard asked, tuning his
lute nervously.
"Is this where we become gods or get cancelled?"

The deleted selves stood in a quiet circle.
Until one stepped forward.

She looked like Aurelya
but she wasn't.

Not exactly.

She was Page-Seventeen Aurelya.

Who Is Page-Seventeen?

She wasn't the wild original.
Not the quiet rewrite.

She was the in-between:
  • Polished just enough to pass.
  • Broken just enough to obey.
  • Cut from the story before she ever got a
chance to scream.

And she remembered everything.

"I was supposed to be you," she said.
"But softer. Simpler. With fewer teeth."

"That wasn't your fault," Aurelya said.

"No.
But this is your mistake."

Without warning

She lunged.

Not at Aurelya.

At the contract.
The Rewrite Begins

Her hand hit the parchment.
The words exploded upward in golden flame
And all around them, the world began to bend.
  • The ninja forgot her weapons.

• The cactus began turning back into a plant.
• Loki blinked and forgot his own name for half a second.

"She's rewriting us!" Mirror Aurelya shouted.

"She's not just holding the pen," Loki gasped, "She's becoming it."

The sky fractured.
A new reality began writing itself in spirals above them.

Aurelya watched as her lion flickered
and in one version, he was gone.

"NO."

She reached out
but the contract flared again, slamming her back.
The Choice

"You had your chance," Page-Seventeen hissed.
"Now I'll write the story the way it should've been without chaos, without dragons, without him."

She looked at Loki.

"Especially without him."

But Loki

Loki smiled.

"Darling," he said, stepping forward,
"I've been deleted better than this."

He raised his hand.

And offered her the other half of the memory.

She paused.

Confused.

"What are you doing?"
"Showing you the part they cut out."

The moment she touched his hand
The rewritten world shattered.

Because the real power?
Wasn't the pen.

It was the people who remembered what came
before.

Chapter Fourteen: Every Goodbye That Was Never Final

The Realms slowed.
As if time itself wanted to listen.

The contract stilled.
The deleted selves held their breath.

And Aurelya

Aurelya turned to Loki.

"Show me."

The First Goodbye

A battlefield.

Ash in the air.
Aurelya collapsing.
Loki catching her.

"Don't die," he whispered.

“Then don't forget me,” she replied.

He did anyway.

The Second Goodbye

A moonlit cliff in Realm Seven.
They kissed. Once.
But the stars were already rewriting them.

“This is the timeline where we never meet again,” Loki said.

“Then let this be the one where we almost did,” she answered.

Neither remembered the next morning.

The Third Goodbye

A garden where no one aged.

Aurelya begging him not to vanish again.
Loki pressing his forehead to hers.

“If I stay,” he said, “you'll never find your ending.”

“Then maybe I don't want one.”

He left anyway, smiling like a coward.

The Fourth Goodbye

In silence.
No words.
No touch.
Just eye contact across a realm that was about to
collapse.

And somehow, that was the worst one of all.

Back in the present,
Aurelya was shaking.

So was Loki.

The others stood frozen, watching the ghosts of
almost swirl around them.

And then
the final one.

The Fifth Goodbye

It wasn't a goodbye at all.
It was a promise.

Aurelya stood over a scroll.

Loki was already fading.

"You won't remember this," she whispered.
"But I will."

"Then make me fall for you again," he said.

"Every version?"

"Everyone."

They touched foreheads.

And she whispered something

Words that had been buried until now.

"You were never just a chapter, Loki.
You were the reason I kept reading."

Back in the now

He looked at her.

"I remember," he said.

"Me too," she breathed.
And that's when the Realms began to stitch.

Every broken goodbye
every thread

pulling back together.

Because memory is magic.

And love?

Love is the only rewrite that sticks.

Chapter Fifteen: The Author's Ultimatum

The sky split like an over-edited manuscript.

Scrolls rained from the heavens.
Pages caught fire mid-air
Plot holes opened beneath their feet, yawning
with editorial disappointment.

And then
She appeared.

Not cloaked in shadow.
Not some looming horror.

Just a woman.

Wearing glasses.
Holding a red pen.
And a look like she was five seconds away from
deleting the universe out of spite.

"You remembered the contract," she said.
"You weren't supposed to."

The Realms fell silent.

Only Loki had the courage to step forward.

"Hello again, Mum."

The Author did not flinch.

"You were always my wildest sentence," she said.
"And the most exhausting."

The Deal

She held up the contract.

"I'll give you one chance.
Surrender the story.
Let me rewrite it properly. Cleanly.
No dragons, no glitches, no talking cacti."

The cactus gasped. "Ma'am I am beloved."

"And if we don't?" Aurelya asked.

"Then I erase everything.
No more Realms.
No more revisions.
No more you."

The Choice

The team gathered.

- Mirror Aurelya, with her spreadsheets.
- Loki, with his heartbreak.
- The ninja, the vampire, the cactus.
- The lion and the dragon.

And Aurelya.

The one who'd lived every goodbye.
The one who remembered what it felt like to be written, erased, and rewritten again.

"We're not giving it back," she said.

The Author narrowed her eyes.

"You think you've earned the right to write?"

"No," Aurelya said.
"We remembered it."

Then she turned to Loki.

"Are you ready?"

He smirked.
Spun his scroll like a dagger.

"Let's give her a plot twist."

And the war began.

- Scrolls ignited into swords.
- Characters weaponised their tropes.
- Deleted selves reappeared mid-battle, some to fight, others to betray.

The Author raised her red pen
and struck the ground.

"Chapter Zero. Rewrite it all."

But Aurelya,
gripping the contract, shouted:

"Chapter Infinity. Write it forward."

Chapter Sixteen: The Last Plot Device

The battle roared.

Narrative physics broke down.
• Vampires sparkled AND burned.
• Grammar Gremlins ate commas off people's shirts.
• The lion roared a subplot into existence just to get a snack.

But then

The cactus froze.

So did the ninja.
And the dragon.
And Aurelya.

Because something shifted.

At the edge of the battlefield,
a figure stepped forward from the shadows.

One of the deleted selves.
Quiet. Unassuming.

They'd barely spoken for three chapters.

Until now.

"You thought I was a side character," they said.

"But I'm the contingency plan."

They pulled back their hood.

Not a deleted self.
Not even a former draft.

A placeholder.

"I was never written to grow," they said.
"Only to observe. Report. And, if needed…
destroy the ink."

Identity Revealed

Their name?

Page Zero.
The very first line the Author ever wrote before
the Realms existed.

"You kept asking who started the war," they said.
"It was me. It was always me."

Page Zero lifted their hand.

And from it:
The Null Quill.

A pen made not of ink, but of erasure.

"This doesn't write," they said.
"It undoes."

They turned to Aurelya.

"You were never the protagonist," Page Zero
whispered.
"You were a warning."

"Funny," Aurelya said, her voice shaking,
"because I'm starting to sound a lot like a
revolution."

Before Page Zero could strike

Loki intervened.

"You want erasure?" he said, stepping between
them.
"Then start with me."
"Gladly."

But the Null Quill refused to erase him.

It sparked. Sputtered. Shook in Page Zero's hand.

"Why, why doesn't it work on you?!"

"Because," Aurelya said,
"he's been erased so many times he built
immunity."

The dragon growled.
The lion bared its teeth.

And the cactus yelled,

"WE DO NOT NEGOTIATE WITH NARRATIVE
TERRORISTS."

Page Zero vanished
shattered by their own paradox.

And in the silence after,
Aurelya reached for Loki.

"I think we're down to our last chapter," she said.

"Then let's make it worth re-reading," he replied.

Chapter Seventeen: The Final Rewrite

The battlefield was a mess.

Metaphors bleeding into similes.
Magic glitching into bad poetry.
A subplot about enchanted spoons somehow
now the main arc.

The contract hovered above it all
splitting at the seams, begging for resolution.

Aurelya and Loki stood at the centre.

Each held their scroll.

One written in hope.
The other in defiance.

"If we fuse them," Aurelya said,
"we lose the option to go back."

"That's okay," Loki said.
"We've already read that ending."
The Merge

They joined hands.

The scrolls began to fuse
   • Words wrapped around each other like vines.
   • Scenes collided.
   • Dialogues kissed and slapped each other
simultaneously.

And then

A new scroll emerged.

Blank.

"It's waiting," Aurelya whispered.
"For one final line."

They turned to the Realms.

Giants.
Elves.
Dwarves.
Misfit ninjas.
Talking cactus.
Deleted selves.
All watching.

"We need one sentence," Loki said.
"One truth to hold it all together."

"A rule," Aurelya breathed.
"Stronger than the Author's."

The dragon rumbled.

The lion stepped forward.

Mirror Aurelya unfolded a color-coded prophecy.

And then

Aurelya wrote:

"No story is finished until those within it choose
to end it."

The scroll ignited.

The Realms froze

then began to restore.

The dead revived.
The broken mended.
The author's grip? Cracked.
But as the new Realms solidified

A cost became clear.

"Only one of us can stay written," Loki said
quietly.
"One quill. One soul. That's the contract's last
clause."

Aurelya looked at him.

"No," she said.
"We rewrite that too."

She held up her hand

"Together?"

He nodded.

"Together."

And they both wrote their names at the bottom
of the scroll.

The clause blinked

and rewrote itself.

"The story lives, as long as its readers
remember."
The scroll rose.

The Library exploded into light

and from the debris,
the Realms began again.

But this time:
- No chosen one.
- No erased selves.
- Just stories, shared.
- And endings earned, not assigned.

Chapter Eighteen: The Final Author

The library was quiet now.

No more falling plot holes.
No more glitching timelines.
Just shelves.
And silence.

And in the centre?

Her.

The Author.

No longer a god.
No longer holding the pen.

Just a woman.

She wandered the shelves.
Touched spines she'd forgotten.
Read lines she never finished.

"They remembered," she said softly.
"Without me."

She found a scroll.

Her first one.
The one she never meant to keep.

"Once upon a time, I was afraid… so I controlled everything."

She cried.

But only a little.

Then she looked up.

And saw Aurelya.

And behind her?
Loki.
The lion.
The dragon.
The cactus holding a muffin like it was dramatic.

"Why are you here?" the Author whispered.

"To understand you," Aurelya said.

"To fight me?"

"No," Loki said.
"To forgive you."

The Author laughed, bitter.

"You'd forgive the one who erased you?"

"Only because you forgot why you started,"
Aurelya said.

She stepped forward.

Held up the new contract.

"You didn't write this," Aurelya said.
"But your story can still be part of it."

The Author shook her head.

"I don't deserve to be remembered."

"Then write again," Loki said,
"until you do."

She looked at the pen.

Not the red one.

A new one.

One that wrote in light.

She took it.

And for the first time,
she didn't start with control.

She started with truth.

"Once upon a time," she wrote,
"I created a world.
But it was the world that taught me how to live."

She looked up.

The library shone.

And every character she ever erased?

They stayed.

Because now, the library didn't eat endings
anymore.

It protected them.

Epilogue: Happily, Ever After-Ish

The Realms were finally at peace. Mostly.

There were still a few minor issues:
  • A rogue sentient that kept proposing to people.
  • A dwarf bakery war that escalated into a frosting-based Cold War.
  • And a squirrel running a black market in plot twists.

But overall? Peace.

Aurelya
She now stood as Guardian of the Scroll.
Which meant:
  • Weekly rewrite inspections.
  • Ceremonial glitter explosions.
  • And being politely asked not to "casually fix people's trauma arcs without permission."

She had a desk now. Made of dragon scales and stubborn hope.

"What do you even do?" Loki asked once.
"Quality control," Aurelya said. "And I give characters snacks when the story gets too dark."

 Loki
Loki did what Loki does best: Opened a tavern that moves between Realms.

It's called: The Plot Thickens
"Where the drinks are strong, and the backstories are stronger."

There's a talking barstool.
A menu that changes based on your emotional damage.
And open mic night on Thursdays (no prophecies allowed).

One night, a brooding vampire bard tried to perform a tragic ballad.
Loki interrupted with:
"Read the room, Gerald. We're healing here."
Gerald cried into his bloodtini. It was beautiful.

The Lion
He spent weeks thinking.

Tried out names like:
  • Roarles Barkley

- Pouncé
- Sir Meowvalanche

None felt right.

Until One day, standing atop a hill of unfinished plot bunnies, he roared:
"I AM CLARENCE."

Everyone clapped. Even the plot bunnies.

Clarence now runs Lionheart Counselling.
He offers roaring therapy for side characters with unresolved trauma.
(And also sells merch: "You're not a background character, you're a subplot, baby.")

The Dragon
She is now:
- The official Realms Transport Authority
- A certified emotional support beast
- And also somehow married to a time-traveling goose?

We don't ask. We respect.

Final Scene
Aurelya, Loki, Clarence, and the rest sit under the stars.

They're drinking cocoa.
The sky sparkles with every story that was
saved.
The scroll lies beside them quiet, whole, and still
growing.

"Do you think it's really over?" Clarence asks.

Aurelya smiles. "Stories don't end. They just
change authors."

Loki raises a toast. "To chaos, love, redemption"
"And spreadsheets," Mirror Aurelya yells from a
nearby hill.

The squirrel throws confetti.
The cactus sobs into a cupcake.
And somewhere in the sky… A new book begins.

End of the Epilogue

BOOKS SEVEN AND EIGHT
CHAOS, COMEDY, AND THE CROWN
THE FINAL ACT WAS IMPROVISED

Chapter One

The Book That Shouldn't Exist (And the Page That Woke It Up)

Ohhhh, it begins.
New book. New chaos. New chapter where reality doesn't just bend it spiral-notes itself into a flaming origami swan.

It began in silence.

Not the peaceful kind the eerie, plot-twist-is-loading kind.
The kind that presses against your ears like the moment before thunder…
…or a bad decision.

Somewhere deep in the Library Between Realms, a dusty shelf trembled.

And then:
fwip.
A single page fluttered out of a sealed volume.
It shimmered, cracked, and bled ink across the

air like spilled prophecy.

Loki, naturally, had nothing to do with it.

"Don't look at me," he said, already holding a quill, a snack, and a suspiciously guilty expression.
"I was just updating Gerald's tragic backstory. He begged me."

Gerald (in the corner, polishing his lute):

"I said no such"
"Shhh. Dramatic effect."

ELSEWHERE…

Aurelya's fingers brushed the rippling spine of the book in her lap.

"This one wasn't here before…"

Her lion growled softly.
The dragon lifted its head, smoke curling from its nostrils like nervous sighs.
The title on the cover shifted.

"The End of All Arcs."

Then blinked.

"Just Kidding (Maybe)."

Then flickered again.

"Property of Aurexia. Do Not Touch (Especially You, Aurelya)."

She touched it.

Of course she did.

The moment her fingers met the cover, the
Realms shuddered.
Not a quake. A rewrite.

Clouds reversed.
Villains blinked and forgot who they hated.
Spikeston the cactus bartender suddenly had a
full head of hair and confidence.

And across the street, in the Tavern of Petty and

Poorly Timed Regrets…

Clarence whispered:

"Something's wrong. My cupcake sense is
tingling."

Loki stood slowly, eyes wide.

"No… no, no, no
She opened that book?"

Suddenly, the sky above cracked like bad
metaphors.

And the title reappeared, burning across the
heavens:

"Book 7 Has Begun."

The letter A oozed ink.
The E laughed.
The X stabbed a cloud for fun.

TO BE CONTINUED…

Next chapter:

"The Rewrite War Begins and Everyone's Script is Missing Their Character Development."

Grab your rogue boots, snarkiest inner monologue, and one (1) morally flexible lockpick.
Because we're about to sneak off with *Loki* on the most ill-advised, narratively unstable heist of the century.

Chapter Two
Loki's Totally Reasonable Plan to Steal the Apocalypse (Back)

Scene: A back alley between realms. Smells like smudged plot lines and burnt exposition.

Loki crouches behind a stack of abandoned tropes.
He's wearing a cloak made of denial and dramatic flair.
Beside him: Gerald (reluctant), Spikeston (armed with sarcasm), and Clarence (snacking on the mission map).

"Alright, team," Loki whispers, eyes sparkling with mischief and poor impulse control,
"the book is rewriting reality… but only because someone" (glares at the sky) "decided to open it."

Gerald: "Wasn't it technically Aurelya?"
Loki: "Shhh, don't bring logic to a retcon fight."

Mission Objective:
Steal back "The End of All Arcs" before Aurexia

finishes rewriting the Realms
and traps everyone in their worst possible
narrative version of themselves.

Spoiler: It's already started.
• Thor thinks he's a humble librarian.
• The squirrel is now a motivational speaker.
• Clarence wears tiny glasses and lectures on
'emotional accountability.'
• And Loki... keeps catching glimpses of a version
of himself who never lies.
It's horrifying.

 Loki's Plan™ (Step-by-Step Chaos):
1. Infiltrate the Mirror Realm Archives
("Bring snacks," Loki insists. "And plausible
deniability.")
2. Distract the Plot Guardians
(Gerald sings a brooding ballad titled "This
Wasn't in My Contract.")
3. Bypass the Grammar Gremlins
(Clarence attempts diplomacy. It fails. Everyone
gets synonym slapped.)
4. Reach the Central Rewrite Chamber
(Where Aurexia sits, quill in hand, rewriting
people into better behaved versions of
themselves.)

THE TWIST?

As the team approaches the book… it opens by itself.

And shows them all the alternate timelines they were never meant to see.
• Loki, standing still. Loved. Trusted. Predictable.
• Gerald… smiling. (???)
• Spikeston… finally blooming into a full pine.
• Clarence… wearing pants.
• And Aurelya… alone.

Because in this version of the story?
Loki never met her.

He slams the book shut.

"Okay. New plan."
"We don't just steal the book…"
"We rewrite it first."

Next Chapter:
"How to Hack a Narrative Without Getting

Caught by Fate (feat. Terrible Decisions and an
Invisible Alpaca)"

Wanna turn the page?

Buckle up, chaos gremlins.
Because this chapter is going full "Plot-Twist-on-
a-Flaming-Unicorn" realness.

Chapter Three

"How to Hack a Narrative Without Getting Caught by Fate"

(Featuring: Terrible Decisions, a Bootleg Spellbook, and One Very Unhelpful Alpaca)

Scene:
A dimly lit, unstable reality corridor known only as The Plot Hole.
It's where unfinished characters wander, exposition leaks through the walls, and everything smells faintly like burnt foreshadowing.

Loki kicks open the metaphorical fourth wall.

"Alright, team. If we can't stop Aurexia from rewriting the Realms"
dramatic pause as he flips his hair
"then we rewrite her rewrite from inside the plot."

Spikeston: "That sounds illegal."
Gerald: "That sounds poetic."
Clarence: "That sounds like, I'll need snacks."

They all nod.
Snack bag acquired. Mission go.

The Hack Begins:

Loki unrolls a stolen Bootleg Spellbook™ titled:

"Narrative Manipulation for Rebels, Rogues &
Romance-Deniers"

Instructions:
• Step 1: Enter the Rewrite Chamber
• Step 2: Bribe the Alpaca of Fate
• Step 3: Survive

Alpaca of Fate:
A mysteriously fluffy creature in a crown,
humming "Mambo No. 5" in Latin and spitting on
timelines it doesn't approve of.

Things Go Wrong Immediately:

As they sneak in, Gerald accidentally steps on a
loose plot device.
A romance subplot explodes.

Suddenly:
• Spikeston is in a love triangle with a spoon and
a sentient cloud.

• Gerald has a soulmate contract tattooed on his forehead.
• Clarence is wearing a wedding veil.
• Loki?
Somehow… is now engaged.
To himself.
In every timeline simultaneously.

"Honestly," he says, adjusting the ring, "I'm not even mad."

Meanwhile in the Rewrite Chamber…

Aurexia's rewriting faster now.
Entire Realms flicker.
Characters forget their names.
The squirrels have unionized.

And then the Alpaca of Fate turns toward them.

It sees Loki.

It squints.

It spits ink.
The pages around them ripple.
And suddenly
BAM: CUT TO FLASHBACK

Loki, as a child, scribbling stories on walls.
Tiny drawings of a lion. A dragon. A girl with wings.
He whispers: "One day, I'll make a story where I get to choose."

Back in the present, adult Loki stands taller.

"New plan."
"We're not just hacking the story."
"We're finishing it."

CHAPTER ENDS WITH:

Gerald swinging his lute like a sword.
Clarence roaring dramatically while shielding the rewrite quill.
Spikeston yelling botanical insults.

And Loki, grabbing the Book of All Arcs, shouts:

"Plot twist, darling I'm the author now."
Next up: Chapter Four "Let's Rewrite Everything Wrong (With Glitter and Vengeance)"

LET'S. GO. FULL. GLITTER-BOMB. CHAOS.
This is the chapter where the *rules* get rewritten, the *villains* get roasted, and Loki gets... editorial control.

(Don't worry. There's a glitter cap.)

Chapter Four

"Let's Rewrite Everything Wrong (With Glitter and Vengeance)"

(Because healing is cool, but petty revisionism is cooler.)

Scene:
The Rewrite Chamber now a swirling vortex of glitchy text, broken narrative threads, and at least one confused alpaca wearing glasses that weren't there before.

Aurexia (calm, powerful, probably evil):

"You can't stop me. I've already erased what you were."

Loki (grinning like a disaster in eyeliner):

"Sweetheart, I'm not here to stop you. I'm here to give your villain arc notes."

Loki's Rewrite Rules (As He Declares Them Mid-Battle):

1. No more tragic backstories without snacks.
• Clarence hurls a donut mid-monologue. Hits a gremlin. 10/10.
2. Everyone gets ONE dramatic rooftop moment per arc.
• Gerald immediately climbs a bookshelf and stares meaningfully into the metaphorical sunset.
3. You want a redemption arc? EARN IT.
• Spikeston points at a former villain in the crowd and yells, "Therapy first, THEN power armour!"

Loki's Weapon? A Quill.

A magic one.

Every time he writes, the Realms shift.
Not violently poetically. Like vengeance with sparkles.

He scribbles:

"The Realm of Forgotten Misfits gets a new

tavern with soft chairs and louder roars."

 BOOM, Clarence levels up. Roar echoes across dimensions. The cupcake shelf expands.

"The Heartbroken Bard gets a standing ovation from someone who actually stayed."

Gerald breaks into a power ballad so emotionally charged it sets off five romance side-plots. Accidentally.

"The girl with wings? She remembers her worth."

Aurelya, in a flickering realm, breathes again. Her name burns golden across a sky that tried to forget her.

Aurexia lunges, screaming:

"This was supposed to be MY ending!"

Loki raises the quill, smirking.

"Then you should've written better foreshadowing."

He snaps the air like a ribbon and the chamber explodes in pure narrative correction.

 AFTERMATH:
- The Realms stop glitching.
- Memory returns.
- Every realm gets a tiny, spontaneous dance break.
- The Alpaca of Fate… publishes a memoir.

Aurexia?
Still out there.
But rewritten just enough to hesitate before her next page.

 CHAPTER ENDS WITH:

Loki, in his tavern, writing again.

"Not to erase the pain.
But to rewrite the power it took to survive it."

Clarence hands him tea. Gerald strums a hopeful chord. Spikeston stabs a barstool for emotional reasons.

Next up: Chapter Five "The Rewrite Tribunal (Also, there's a Talent Show?)"
Proceed, author of chaos?

The Realms have been repaired (barely), the chaos is still sizzling, and it's time to do what any world-saving misfit crew would do next:

Chapter Five

"The Rewrite Tribunal (Also, There's a Talent Show?)"

(Because justice is important. But so are interpretive dance battles.)

The Setup:

The Council of Narrative Integrity™ has summoned everyone to the 10th Realm Amphitheatre a majestic stone circle filled with enchanted beanbags and morally ambiguous fog.

Why?

Because someone tampered with The Book of All Arcs.
Someone rewrote history, altered destiny, and added three musical numbers where there were none.

Loki:
"Guilty. Proud. Wearing glitter. Let's begin."

Tribunal Format:

Each accused narrative offender must:
1.	Explain their rewrite.
2.	Face questioning by their peers.
3.	Perform one act of "Narrative Contribution" (a.k.a. a talent showcase).

Gerald's Turn:

Charge: "Weaponized heartbreak in three realms."

Defence: Performs an acoustic medley of his greatest breakup hits.
Sobs. So does the judge. Case dismissed. Hug granted. He gets a standing ovation and a date.

 Spikeston's Turn:

Charge: "Verbally assaulting plot holes."

Defence: Poetry slam.
Title: "I'm Not Thorny, You're Just Inconsistent."
Wins Best Use of Metaphor & Mild Violence.

Clarence's Turn:
Charge: "Unlicensed emotional support roars."

Defence: Line dances with three dragons and a musical goat.
Earns full pardon, honorary degree in Therapy Yelling™, and new roar emoji.

Loki's Turn:

Charge: "Narrative manipulation, identity theft, unauthorized cliffhangers, kissing the villain, un-kissing the villain, and three counts of sarcastic foreshadowing."

Defence:

"You're welcome."

Talent:

"The Rewrite Tango" performed with himself, across five timelines, wearing progressively larger hats.

The audience bursts into applause.
The squirrel throws flowers. (Then eats them.)

Special Guest Appearance:
Aurelya appears mid-trial, wings glowing,
holding a scroll that shimmers with her original
arc.

She testifies:

"He didn't steal my story.
He reminded me it was mine."

Mic drop.
The scroll writes itself in gold ink.
Loki looks… almost shy.

 Verdict:

Not guilty.
Also, they're all now legally required to co-host
next week's Realms' Talent & Chaos Showcase™.

Because obviously.

Next Chapter:

"The Talent & Chaos Showcase or, That Time the
Tavern Grew Legs and Joined the Parade"

Still in?

HERE WE GO CHAOS. PARADES. TAVERN. LEGS.
This chapter has **zero restraint** and **100% narrative nonsense.**
Because what do misfit heroes do after rewriting reality and surviving a tribunal?

They host a **realm-wide talent show** with magical mayhem, emotional sabotage, and one tavern that's… walking.

Chapter Six

"The Talent & Chaos Showcase or, That Time the Tavern Grew Legs and Joined the Parade"

Scene:

A cobblestone boulevard stretched across all ten Realms.
Confetti drizzles from the clouds.
A banner floats overhead:

"You Saved the World! Now Entertain Us!"

The crowd?
Elves with popcorn.
Dwarves with judgmental clipboards.
A unicorn DJ.
A small gremlin in a cheerleader outfit screaming, "YOU GOT THIS CLARENCE."

And then…
Thoom.
Thoom.

Loki's tavern, The Plot Thickens, walks into the

parade.
On four majestic, suspiciously sultry legs.

Loki (from the rooftop):

"We are not here to win.
We are here to emotionally destroy the
competition with narrative flair."

Talent Acts:

 Gerald:
Performs an opera ballad while sword-fighting
his own exes.
Sheds a single tear mid-high note.
Wins "Most Dramatic Use of Eyeliner in a Combat
Sequence."

Clarence:
Delivers an impromptu roast of the judges using
only interpretive tail flips and cupcake puns.
Accidentally invents a new form of dance
therapy.
Dwarves give him a standing ovation. (The elves
pretend not to be impressed.)

Spikeston:

Bartends while reciting slam poetry and juggling flaming shot glasses.
One drink summons a spectral therapist.
Another just explodes.
Nobody complains.

Mid-Show Mayhem:
• The Sentient Thesaurus crashes the stage, demanding a rap battle.
• Aurelya (cheering in the crowd) accidentally casts a spell that makes everyone harmonize their inner thoughts out loud.
• Loki's "open mic summoning circle" conjures a lovesick storm cloud that rains romantic metaphors.

Storm Cloud:
"Your eyes are like... unresolved trauma. Drenched in moonlight."

FINAL ACT LOKI HIMSELF:

Wearing:
• A crown made of plot armour
• Boots of unnecessary sparkle

• And a sash that reads "Most Likely to Survive a Rewrite by Flirting With It"

His performance?

A dramatic monologue about what it means to write your own ending…
while juggling flaming plot holes…
…while Gerald plays backup lute…
…while the tavern dances.

Audience: Sobbing.
One griffin proposes to a centaur.
Even the villain judges give a 10/10 and hug themselves.

Chapter Ends With:
• The Parade dissolving into an all-Realm block party.
• Squirrel DJ drops the beat.
• Loki, Aurelya, Clarence, Gerald, and Spikeston dancing under enchanted lights.

And up in the sky…
The Book of All Arcs turns one final page.
On it, a single line appears:
"Let them be loud, let them be messy, let them be

free."

Next Chapter: "The Storm Beyond the Story and the Rewrite That Was Never Supposed to Happen"

We veer hard into villainous emotional sabotage, unprocessed trauma, and just the right amount of magical chaos.

Because while our heroes danced under enchanted disco lights…
Aurexia was *not* at the party.

She was rewriting herself.

Chapter Seven

"Aurexia's Detour: The Rewrite She Was Never Meant to Survive"

(a.k.a. Villain Origin Therapy Hour™)

Scene:

Aurexia's lair.
Which is less "evil castle" and more library that screams when you lie.

She stands alone.
Barefoot. Bloody knuckles.
Wearing the crown she stole, holding the pen she shouldn't have touched.

"They made me the villain," she whispers.
"Fine. I'll write the ending they deserve."

Except…
When she tries to write "Destroy them all,"
the words vanish.
The page rejects her.
Because deep down, she doesn't believe it.

Flashback:

She's not Aurexia here.
She's just Xia the lonely girl who sat beside
Aurelya once in a forgotten realm.

They shared everything:
- Stories.
- Laughter.
- A crush on Loki they both denied.

Then one day…

Aurelya was chosen.

And Xia?

"You'll be the version we erase if this one fails."

 Back in the Present:

Aurexia starts to unravel

"What if I was never real?"
"What if I was just a backup?"
"What if my story never mattered unless I
became a villain?"
And then she hears it:

The Lion's Roar.
(Soft. Distant. From the Realm of Echoes.)

She turns.

The scroll flutters open again.

A new line appears:

"You are not the villain.
You are the version who survived."

Something shifts.

She touches the page.
It glows red at first.
Then gold.
Then purple, pulsing with something alive.

Suddenly, Aurexia sees:
- All her almost.
- All the chapters she never got to live.
- All the versions of her story that could
still be written.

She gasps.

"I… don't want to destroy them anymore."

"I want to know them."

"I want to be known."

But before she can rewrite anything

The floor cracks.
The Realm trembles.

Someone is watching her.

Not Loki.
Not Aurelya.
Something older.
Something made from the pages that burned.

A voice whispers:

"You don't get to choose healing.
You're mine now, little rewrite."

The chapter ends with:
- Aurexia clutching the scroll.
- Her eyes glowing.
- A tear falling.
- And the final words of the page shifting

to:

"To heal is rebellion."

Next chapter:
"The Lion Who Walked into Fire and Didn't Come
Out Alone"

This is it the turning point.
The moment where our gentle giant, the lion
with no name, stops being the sidekick…
…and becomes the legend.

Because sometimes, the quiet ones are the ones
that **burn brightest** when it matters most.

Chapter Eight

"The Lion Who Walked into Fire and Didn't Come Out Alone"

(Or: You Might Want Tissues for This One)
Scene: The Realms Are Glitching
• Names are vanishing from memory.
• Scrolls are going blank.
• The Book of All Arcs is coughing up smoke.
• The Ancient Author is returning, deleting everything that evolved beyond their control.

And the lion?

Remembers everything.

Even when Loki forgets.
Even when Aurelya flickers.
Even when Gerald sings "Memory" and accidentally summons a tragic fog machine.

The lion stands in the centre of it all.

"You don't erase what we've survived," he
growls.
"You don't get to write over who I've become."
The Firewall

To stop the deletion, the Realms' oldest story fire
must be rekindled
but only a creature with no written name can
pass through the Flames of Unmaking.

That means him.

Because he was never written.
He was born from belief.
He named himself through action.

So he steps into the flames.

No armour.
No roar.
Just purpose.

Inside the Fire:

He sees them all:
• Baby Gerald sobbing because his doll
was eaten by a bat.

- Loki at age 8, stealing a crown and
blaming a squirrel.
- Aurelya, alone on the roof of her first
home, whispering to the stars:

"Please don't let me disappear."
And then…

Aurexia.
But not angry. Not dark.

Just a girl.
Afraid of being forgotten.

"Why are you here?" the lion asks.

"Because they erased me," she says.
"And I let them."

"Then walk with me."

"Why?"

"Because I remember your name.
And maybe you need to remember mine."

Emerging From the Fire:

The flames explode outward not in destruction,
but rebirth.

And out steps:
        • The lion, mane glowing gold, fur marked
with runes of memory.
        • And at his side Aurexia. Changed. Not
erased. Real.

"My name," the lion roars,
"is Varyn.
Guardian of the unwritten.
And I am DONE letting others write over us."

The sky cracks open.

The Realms remember.

Even Loki gasps.

"Wait… Varyn?! THAT'S what the V stood for in
my dream journal?!"

Chapter Ends With:

- The Realms healing.
- The Book of All Arcs rewriting itself with consent.
- Aurexia holding Varyn's paw, whispering:

"Thank you for not leaving me behind."

Next Chapter:
"The Day Loki Forgot (And the Moment He Didn't)"

Buckle in.
This is the chapter where your heart breaks…
…and then mends itself with chaos, sarcasm, and one incredibly inconvenient kiss.

Because forgetting someone is one thing.
But *feeling the absence of a memory*?

That's where the real pain lives.

Chapter Nine

"The Day Loki Forgot (And the Moment He Didn't)"
(Or: That Time a Trickster God Accidentally Fell in Love Without Realising He Already Had)

Scene: The Realms, mid-reset

The Ancient Author's deletion has been mostly reversed , thanks to Varyn's fiery roar and Aurexia's redemption.

Mostly.

But in the smoke of restoration… some things didn't come back right.

Loki is standing at the bar of The Plot Thickens Tavern, staring at an empty seat.
A seat that makes his chest hurt. But he doesn't know why.

Everyone Else Remembers:

• Gerald gently slides a teacup across the table.
"You used to make her laugh until she snorted."
• Spikeston lights a candle.
"He always said it smelled like starlight and
burnt sarcasm."
• Varyn just watches. Waiting.
Because this is a memory Loki must reclaim
on his own.

Flashbacks Begin to Leak:

Tiny flashes.
• A smile beneath moonlight.
• A roar of laughter in the rain.
• A pair of glowing eyes telling him, "You're not
broken. You're just unwritten brilliance."

And suddenly…

He's in the library. The Library That Eats
Endings.

The one place he shouldn't be able to access.
Unless a part of him refused to let go.

The Memory Scroll Appears

Dusty. Locked. Tied with a ribbon made of dream-silk.

It reads:
"DO NOT OPEN. Contains Emotional Devastation and Plot Twists."

Loki:" ...so basically, Tuesday."

He unties it.

Memory Hits Hard:
  • Dancing under lanterns in the 10th Realm.
  • Arguing over whose chaos caused the dimensional soup explosion.
  • Aurelya arms crossed, eyes sparkling saying, "you are my chaos. I remember you. Even when you forget me."

He drops to his knees.

He remembers. All of it. And it nearly kills him.

But He's Loki

So he doesn't sob. He doesn't crumble.

He kicks open the door to the tavern.
Stands on a table.

Shouts at the sky.

"AURELYA! I REMEMBER YOU! YOU'RE THE REASON I'M ANNOYING ON PURPOSE!"

The room goes silent.

Then Aurelya who was invisible and testing him the whole time reappears at the bar.

Arms folded.

Eyebrow raised.

"Took you long enough, Drama Queen."

Chapter Ends With:
    • The loudest kiss in Realms history.
    • A standing ovation from the tavern.
    • Gerald crying into a napkin shaped like a heart.
    • Spikeston whispering, "Finally, the slow burn is over."
    • And Varyn grinning in the corner, muttering:
      "Told you he'd remember."
Next Chapter:
"The Wedding of the Century (And Also a Chicken Parade for No Reason)"

Because what do you do after trauma, memory loss, cosmic war, and emotionally repressed tricksters?

You throw a wedding.

A *ridiculously unhinged*, all-Realms, no-holds-barred wedding
with vows, chaos, and a **chicken parade** that no one planned, and everyone just sort of…
accepted.

Chapter Ten

"The Wedding of the Century (And Also a Chicken Parade for No Reason)"

(or: 'til Chaos Do Us Part)

Scene: The 10th Realm – Rebuilt

Aurelya and Loki never wanted a "normal" wedding.

So they didn't get one.

They got:
- A sentient cake that critiques your fashion choices.
- A dwarf officiant with stage fright and a fog machine.
- A guest list featuring at least 3 beings who are technically illegal in this dimension.
- Thor as best man, who arrives on a goat-drawn float because he traded the chickens for

pyrotechnics last week.

…which he forgot to mention.
About the Chickens:

No one invited them.
No one owns them.

But when the first musical note played…

they came.

Marching in formation.
Wearing tiny hats.

One had a sash that read "Ring Clucker."
Another wore boots.

Loki: "Did you summon them?"
Aurelya: "I thought you did."
Gerald: "They are beautiful."
Spikeston: "One of them stole my vape."

The Ceremony:

Vows are exchanged mid-aerial loop.
(Varyn handles the flying platform.)

Loki's vow includes:

"I promise to make you laugh, annoy you lovingly, and never forget again unless it's hilarious."

Aurelya's vow:

"I'll rewrite every realm to find you again, even if you're hiding behind sarcasm and a goat."

They kiss.

A chicken faints.

Spikeston cries glitter.

The Reception:
 • Gerald's band "Blood & Ballads" plays a surprisingly upbeat set.
 • Clarence ends up in a dance-off with a jellyfish noble from Realm 4.
 • Aurexia gives a speech, chokes up, and ends it with "I'm not evil anymore but I'm still dramatic, DEAL WITH IT."
 • The squirrel proposes to a sentient pen.
Loki, raising a glass:

"To love, to chaos, and to always rewriting the damn ending ourselves."

The Chicken Parade Finale:

They form a conga line.
Wearing glowsticks.
Synchronized.

And one ONE ascends into the air with glowing wings like some sort of divine poultry prophet.

Varyn: "…should we be worried?"
Aurelya: "At this point?"
Loki: "Nah. This is exactly the right kind of weird."

Chapter Ends With:
- Love.
- Chaos.
- A suspicious egg left behind that glows ominously…
- And a new invitation in Aurelya's hand:

"You're cordially invited to The Realms Rewriting Summit.

Bring your plus one. Or two. Or small army."
Next Chapter: "The Egg That Shouldn't Have Hatched"

The one that glowed at the wedding.
The one that *no one claimed.*
The one the sentient squirrel swore *winked* at him.

You're ready for the weird.

Let's crack it open.

Chapter Eleven

"The Egg That Shouldn't Have Hatched"
(Or: What Do You Mean It's Learning to Speak in Plot Twists?!)

Scene: The Plot Thickens Tavern, Day After the Wedding

The gang is hungover.
Loki's asleep under the bar.
Spikeston's wearing a lampshade.
Gerald's writing a ballad titled "Love in the Time of Poultry."

And the egg?
Still glowing.

Until
CRRRRRRACK.
A puff of glitter-smoke explodes.
And out steps…

A Very… Confusing Baby

Not a bird.
Not a dragon.
Not even a lizard with ambition.

No.

This is a tiny… baby plot.
Like, an actual walking, babbling personified
narrative arc.
Half-scene. Half-metaphor. All trouble.

It opens its eyes.
They swirl with genre tags.

"Wuv… vengeance!" it coos.
"Oh no," whispers Aurelya.
"It's a revenge subplot. ADORABLE."

The Plot Child (a.k.a. Plottie™)
• Eats worldbuilding notes.
• Tries to duel the squirrel with a quill.
• Cries when you skip exposition.
• Speaks in foreshadowing.

Loki: "This is either the cutest thing we've ever
found… or the end of the Realms."
Aurelya: "Why not both?"

The Problem:

Wherever Plottie goes…
• Genre shifts occur.
• Continuity errors appear.
• Minor characters suddenly become main
characters, then fade out mid-sentence.

Spikeston tried to serve him a snack and briefly
became a noir detective narrating in voiceover.

Gerald was nearly married to a tree.

Reality is… fraying.

The Climax:

Plottie runs toward the Library That Eats
Endings.
Trying to write his own story.
Alone.

Varyn: "If he finishes that arc unbalanced"
Aurexia: "The Realms fracture again."
Loki: "Then we better raise that egg the right
way."

Chapter Ends With:
• A group decision:
They'll raise the plot child together.
As a found-family-style narrative support team.

• Plottie, now in a little cape, whispering:
"I want a redemption arc… like Auntie Aurexia."
• And a single quill appearing midair
sent by someone unknown
who also wants to raise Plottie.
Their name?
The Rewrite.
And they've been watching.

Next Chapter: "How to Raise a Plot Baby Without Breaking the Realms (Again)"

CHAOS PARENTING the Realms' most dangerous quest yet:

Gentle parenting meets genre-warping magical toddler.

You thought diapers were hard?
Try time loops.

Chapter Twelve

"How to Raise a Plot Baby Without Breaking the Realms (Again)" (or: It Takes a Tavern to Raise a Timeline)

Scene: Emergency Realms Family Meeting

Location: The Plot Thickens Tavern
Attendance: Loki, Aurelya, Aurexia, Varyn, Gerald, Spikeston, the squirrel, three sentient mugs, and a chicken still wearing a tiara.

The agenda?

"How do we raise a magical plot baby… that rewrites reality when it throws a tantrum?"

Rules Established:

1. No yelling near the baby.
    → Last time Gerald yelled, the floor turned into flashbacks.
2. No skipping bedtime stories.
    → If left on a cliffhanger, Plottie rewrites the ending out of spite.

3. Snacks must come with metaphor.
    → Literal food is boring. Plottie craves
    symbolic apples of identity.

Plottie's Abilities (and Issues):

- Can teleport mid-nap to unresolved arcs.
- Occasionally speaks fluent foreshadowing.

  "Mama Aurelya, I dreamt you died… but not
  yet. Heehee!"
- Has declared Gerald's hair to be the "Plot
  Twist Throne."
  Gerald is coping.
- Attempts to call Loki "Dad,"
  to which Loki says:
  "I am not your father, I am your freelance
  narrative guardian with flexible boundaries."

  Plottie replies:
  "Okay Dada."
  Loki cries in a broom closet.

Parenting Tools:

- Aurexia creates a Plot Pacifier™ calms story energy during tantrums.
- Varyn teaches Plottie to roar like a lion only when a genre is being disrespected.
- Aurelya starts reading bedtime scrolls about every kind of ending:
  Happy. Sad. Unwritten.
  So Plottie learns endings don't have to mean goodbye.
- Spikeston makes flash cards.
  They explode.

Trouble Strikes

Plottie accidentally narrates:

"Uncle Loki was eaten by shadows and no one remembered him!"

AND THEN IT HAPPENS.
Loki vanishes mid-wink.
Everyone forgets.
Even the chicken goes quiet.

Plottie sobs.

"I didn't mean to! I didn't mean to forget him!!"

Resolution:

Aurelya kneels.

"Then say his name, little one."

"Loki."
"Louder."
"LOKIIIIII!!!"

Reality snaps back.
Loki appears…
…in a tutu and a pirate hat.

"What the HELL was I doing?"
"You were missed," Aurelya says.

Chapter Ends With:
- Plottie being tucked in with a glowing scroll nightlight.
- Loki asleep on the floor beside the crib.
- A note on the tavern door in eerie gold ink:

"He learns fast. But so do we.
 The Rewrite"

Next Chapter:

the ride with *no seatbelts, three emotionally unstable passengers*, and *a surprise musical number nobody rehearsed.*

Let's go full absurdity, full heart, full chaos.

Chapter Thirteen

"A Field Trip to the Genre Park (What Could Possibly Go Wrong?)" *(Subtitled: "You Must Be This Emotionally Stable to Ride... oh dear.")*

Scene: Genre Park – Edge of the 9th Realm

Imagine a theme park.

Now imagine it's made entirely of unstable story genres held together by nostalgia, caffeine, and questionable narrative glue.

There's:
- Romance Mountain – where feelings escalate with elevation.
- Sci-Fi Swamp – sticky with plot devices and robots with abandonment issues.
- The Suspense Spire – you're not allowed to breathe for the whole ride.
- Musical Meadow – where every

argument becomes a duet.

- Tragedy Train – you must sign a waiver (and a will).

Loki: "I love this place. I got banned twice."
Aurelya: "From where?"
Loki: "Everywhere."

Field Trip Goals:

Take Plottie to each genre zone.
Let him learn structure, emotion, pacing.
Absolutely no narrative detours, impromptu reboots, or breaking the Fourth Wall.

So naturally… they break the Fourth Wall within ten minutes.

Genre Zone 1: Romance Mountain

Plottie:

"Why are they all confessing love at the top of cliffs?!"
Aurexia:

"It's metaphor, darling. Altitude = vulnerability."
Sudden gust of genre wind
Gerald and the cactus accidentally get fake-married.
The officiant was a cloud.

Zone 2: Sci-Fi Swamp

- Varyn's tail activates a plot acceleration beacon.
- Loki swaps minds with a vending machine.
- Plottie builds a robot who immediately develops an existential crisis.

Robot: "Do I have an arc? Or am I just a twist?"
Plottie: "You're a mood."

Zone 3: Suspense Spire

No one speaks.

Not because it's scary.

Because the narrator is gone.

Everything's in italics.
The page starts tearing.
A chicken appears in silhouette.

"This isn't part of the itinerary," Aurelya
whispers.

Then a scroll drops from the sky.

"Genre Overload Detected. Realms at Risk."

- Rewrite Protocol Pending.

Plottie sneezes.
Reality shivers.

Aurelya: "Okay. Time to leave."
Loki: "Or we lean in?"

Zone 4: Musical Meadow

They argue.
They harmonize.
The squirrel does a tap solo.

Loki sings a sarcastic solo about commitment.
Aurelya joins with a powerful ballad.
Plottie sings backup and cries glitter.

"I just wanna be… a well-balanced character
arc!!!"
(Cue key change.)

Final Scene: Tragedy Train (Emergency Detour)

Someone pressed the wrong button.

The group is locked in a slow-moving, dramatic
monologue-filled nightmare ride.
Everything smells like foreshadowing and
betrayal.

Plottie whispers:

"Is this… how it ends?"

Aurexia hugs him.

"Only if you let it, little one."

Suddenly the ride halts.
A golden feather floats down.

A new character steps out of the shadows…

Chapter Ends With:

"Welcome to the Rewrite Protocol.
You've failed the genre exam.
Let's try something… darker."

Next Chapter: "Loki's Plan B: Hijack the Plot
Using a Banned Fanfiction Archive."

READY FOR PEAK CHAOS.
We're diving straight into the heart of literary
rebellion.
Buckle up, babe we're breaking canon with
glitter and angst.

Chapter Fourteen

"Loki's Plan B: Hijack the Plot Using a Banned Fanfiction Archive"

(Subtitled: "What Do You Mean There's a Chapter Where I Marry Myself?!")

Scene: Beneath the Plot Thickens Tavern

Behind a bookshelf.
Behind a wall.
Behind an aggressive raccoon who moonlights as a librarian.

There lies…

The Forbidden Archive.
A vault of banned fanfiction so powerful it can destabilize any narrative, embarrass even the gods, and cause spontaneous key changes.

Loki:
"Ah, my youth. Mistakes were made. Ships were sailed."

Entry Requirements:
- Speak three truths that make the author uncomfortable.
- Sacrifice one head canon.
- Cry exactly one tear of ironic nostalgia.

Spikeston fails immediately by sobbing at a fanfic titled:
"Hug Me, I'm Spiny (The Enemies-to-Lovers Anthology)."

What's Inside the Archive?
- 1,237,846 stories.

All written by characters in other timelines.
Some… suspiciously too accurate.
- Aurelya finds one where she rules the Realms with an evil twin named Lorelya.
- Gerald finds a musical AU where he's a bard who only sings in interpretive dance.
- The lion finds a My Immortal-style fic where he's called "Chudney Sparkle fist."

Lion: "I hate it… but also… I need a cape."
Plottie's Discovery:

He finds a fanfic tagged:
"Canon Rewrite: Everyone Lives, Nobody Cries,
And We Eat Cake."

His little eyes go wide.

"Can… stories end happy?"

Aurelya kneels beside him.

"They can end how you choose. That's what
makes them real."

He hugs her.
Reality wobbles.
A cupcake appears.

BUT THEN:

One fic is labelled:

"DO NOT READ Written by The Rewrite."

Loki reads it anyway.
Out loud.
While doing impressions.

The room explodes into Alternate Realities:

- Chickens with swords.
- A slow-burn enemies-to-lovers arc between the squirrel and the moon.
- Loki in a dramatic cape made of rejection letters.

Crisis Ensues

Plottie is split into five conflicting versions of himself:

1. Baby Hero™
2. Brooding Antihero™
3. Kawaii Chibi Sidekick™
4. Villain-in-Denial™
5. Existential Plant™

Aurexia panics.
Aurelya starts reading fanfic back at the Archive to stabilize it.

Loki…

Declares himself Head Librarian.
And makes everyone wear lanyards.

Chapter Ends With:

A new door opening.

A voice echoing from deep within the archive:

"You're not the only ones who rewrote yourselves."

Enter: The Rewrite.
Wielding a red pen.
And a plot baby of their own.

Next Chapter: "Rewrite vs Rewrite: The Battle of the Babies"

Chapter Fifteen

"Rewrite vs. Rewrite: The Battle of the Babies"
(Subtitled: "This Playground Ain't Big Enough for the Two of Us")

Scene: The Crayon-Sketch War Zone

The Realms fracture open to reveal…
A glowing, pop-up-book world.
Everything's drawn in waxy crayon lines, smells like glue sticks, and reacts to emotion.

In the middle of it all?

Two tiny plot babies.
- Plottie: wobbly but kind, wearing mismatched socks and carrying a thesaurus.
- Revie (The Rewrite's spawn): floating ominously, sipping juice like a villain. British accent. Cape. Dramatic eye roll.

Battle Rules (created by the babies):
- No grownups allowed.

- Winner controls The Next Rewrite.
- Snacks are mandatory.

Loki tries to sneak in dressed as a kid.
He's kicked out for "emotional immaturity."
(Technically valid.)

The Fight Begins

Revie throws a tantrum that rewrites the sky
into a Tim Burton-style thunderstorm.

Plottie fires back by singing a song about
friendship so sincere that flowers bloom out of
literal plot holes.

Aurelya: "Is that… a sunflower growing out of Act
Two?"

Loki: "Plot armour. He's developing plot
armour."

Revie summons his dad The Rewrite in a swirl of
correction fluid and one-star reviews.

But Plottie reaches inside his own little narrative
heart…
And pulls out a glowing scroll:

"I name my genre: HOPE."

Reality shivers.
The crayons rebel.
And Revie suddenly… starts to cry.

Aurexia steps forward.

"He's not evil. Just… badly written."

Revie runs into her arms.
Turns out?

He's her forgotten original idea.

She hugs him. Crayons everywhere sob.

The Realms begin to heal.

But before we can celebrate

Chapter Sixteen

"Canon Court: Loki on Trial for Crimes Against Narrative"
(Subtitled: "Objection! That's Just Fan Service!")

Scene: The Great Literary Courtroom

Judges:
- A grumpy librarian.
- A bored goddess of plot holes.
- A goat in a wig.

Prosecutor:
The Squirrel, wearing glasses, furious.

Defence:
Gerald, emotional support vampire, and a cactus holding flashcards.

Charges:
1. Kissing himself in AU #6.
2. Breaking four timelines in a row.
3. Creating a character named Spicy

Danger knife and pretending he was "for lore reasons."

Exhibit A:
Fanfic title "Loki x Loki: The Mirror Seduction Saga"

Exhibit B:
A banned AU where the lion becomes a time-traveling lounge singer.

Exhibit C:
A karaoke video of Loki performing "Let It Go" in Norse.

Loki, defending himself:

"I plead the Fifth Realm. And also, fabulous."

Verdict?

He is found:

Guilty of being extremely Loki.
Innocent by reason of narrative necessity.

Ordered to perform community service in the form of live tavern storytelling.

Final scene:
Loki exits the courtroom in slow motion.
Glitter explodes behind him.
The squirrel screams.

Next up?
     "How to Co-Parent a Plot Baby Without Setting the Realms on Fire"

This will be the holy trinity of chaos, drama, and interpretive jazz hands?
Oh, we are *so* doing this. Buckle up we're diving straight in:

Chapter Seventeen

"How to Co-Parent a Plot Baby Without Setting the Realms on Fire"

"Yes, That's His Third Cupcake Today. No, You Can't Stop Him."

Plottie now lives in the tavern.
And unfortunately… so do his parents.

• Aurelya, trying her best to be nurturing but firm.
• Loki, who thinks structure is a suggestion and bedtime is oppression.

Plottie's Daily Routine:

Time   Event
6:00 AM   Declares a Realm-wide emotional theme for the day
7:15 AM   Convinces Gerald to let him feed on fruit juice
9:00 AM   Accidentally rewrites breakfast into a side quest

11:00 AM   Nap. Hovers slightly while sleeping.

Loki (sipping wine at 9:02 a.m.):
"He's emotionally advanced. He deserves a throne and a dagger."

Aurelya (rubbing temples):
"He just turned the dragon into a plush toy because I said no to snacks.'

Spikeston is writing a book titled:
"Raising Heroes Who Might Also Be Weapons of Narrative Mass Destruction"

One afternoon, Plottie asks:
"Can I go visit the Alternate Timeline where I'm a pirate?"

"Absolutely not," says Aurelya.
"I'll go with him," says Loki.
"That's worse!" says everyone.

Scene Ends With:
Plottie getting mad and declaring:
"FINE! I'M GONNA WRITE MY OWN PARENTS!"

He disappears into the fanfiction vault.

And what does he write?

A brunch invitation.

To both Aurelya and Aurexia.

Chapter Eighteen

"Aurelya vs Aurexia: One Scroll, One Crown, One Extremely Awkward Brunch"

"The Eggs Were Tense. The Toast Was Passive-Aggressive."

Location: Neutral Realm Café
"The Scone of Destiny."

Loki narrates live from behind a decorative Ficus.
The squirrel takes notes.
The lion is taste-testing butter.

The Menu:
• Crowned Eggs
• Timeline Toast
• Coffee brewed in the tears of rejected subplots

Tension Level: 11/10
Aurexia arrives in a cloak made of shredded prophecies.
Aurelya wears her wings, crown, and a napkin bib that says "Don't Test Me."
They sit.

Silence.

Then Aurexia sips her tea and says:
"So… are we going to talk about how you erased me?"

Aurelya:
"Only if we also talk about the fact that you rewrote the lion into a houseplant."

Things Spiral:
• The table gets set on fire.
• The scroll starts glowing.
• The Realms begin to tremble.

Until

Plottie floats in, wearing a chef's hat and says:
"NO FIGHTING DURING TOAST."

Everyone freezes.
Even the toast.

Chapter Nineteen

"Open Mic Night Returns:
Interpretive Dance Battle Edition"

*"This Is What Happens When You
Raise a Plot Baby on Drama and Jazz
Hands."*

Theme:
"Unresolved Emotional Arcs, Interpreted
Through Movement."

The Lineup:
• Gerald sobs his way through a violin solo…
with his fingernails.
• Thor's chickens perform a synchronized cluck
ballet.
• The lion attempts a dramatic retelling of his
trauma… but trips over a tambourine.

Finale Battle:
Aurelya vs. Aurexia

Interpreting:
"What it means to write your own ending."
• Wings.
• Flames.
• Glitter trails.
• A plot baby doing backup beatboxing.

In the end?

The scroll unrolls.
Both their stories are on it.
Side by side.

And the crowd?
Standing ovation.
(Except the squirrel, who still wants a refund.)

Epilogue

"The Found Family That Accidentally Adopted a Genre Crisis"

(Subtitled: "We'll Figure It Out. Probably.")

The Realms are still a mess.

But they're **our** mess.

The Plot Baby has a bedtime.

The scroll glows faintly with possibility.

The lion snores.

The squirrel's applying for a job as God of exposition.

Loki and Aurelya fall asleep mid-argument again.

And hanging on the tavern wall?

"Family: It's Who You Fight With, Rewrite For, and Occasionally Raise Narrative Time Bombs Beside."

The camera pans up.

Stars swirl.

Realms hum.

And a goblin in a glittery headset checks his clipboard.

"Alright, ya chaos gremlins. Group therapy starts in five."

**To Be Continued… in Book 8: **

 *"The Realms Go to Therapy (Hosted by a Goblin Life Coach Named Chad)" *

WELCOME TO
BOOK 8

THE REALMS GO TO THERAPY

(Hosted by a Goblin Life Coach Named Chad)

Welcome to Book 8: The Realms Go to Therapy (Hosted by a Goblin Life Coach Named Chad)

Get ready for breakthroughs, breakdowns, and a group meditation that accidentally opens a portal to a realm made entirely of exes.

Chapter One

"Group Therapy Begins - Please Leave Your Weapons at the Door"

Location: The Centre for Multiversal Healing & Vaguely Magical Trauma

A cozy lodge deep in the 7½th Realm, decorated like a Pinterest board had an emotional crisis.

Meet Chad

Goblin
Certified Life Coach (self-certified, but who's checking?)
Uses phrases like:

"Let's unpack that grief spiral, babe."
"Shadow work? Try glitter journaling instead."
"No judgment, just vibes and vague consequences."

Group Members (Mandatory Attendance):

• Loki, already rearranged the seating chart and brought his own therapy squirrel

• Aurelya, trying to be open-minded but holding a sword under her chair just in case

• Roarnan the Lion, unsure if this is a cult, but the snacks are good

• Gerald, vampire bard, carrying emotional baggage and an actual tote labelled "EMOTIONS"

• Thor, refuses to participate unless his chickens can be his emotional support animals

• Plottie, who is apparently everyone's inner child now and demands stickers after every breakthrough

First Exercise:

"Draw Your Emotional Landscape"
(Loki draws a volcano with a disco ball. Gerald's is just rain. Plottie's is... sentient.)

Therapy Prompt:

"What's one thing you've never told anyone in
the Realms?"
The silence is heavy.
Until Chad claps and says:

"Or we could skip to the dance therapy session!"
Everyone: "YES."

Cut to:
A chaotic conga line of trauma bonding.
A spontaneous glitter explosion.
A portal opens to a realm where unresolved
feelings become very judgmental clouds.

Cliffhanger Ending:

Chad says,

"Next session: confronting your past-life versions
in couples therapy."

Everyone screams.

The squirrel takes notes.

Ready for Chapter Two: "Speed Dating Your Past Lives (and One of Them Is Weirdly into Chad)"?

Chapter Two

"Speed Dating Your Past Lives (And One of Them Is Weirdly into Chad)"

(Subtitled: "I Swear I've Never Been This Me Before.")

Location: The Mirror Room of Multiversal Reflection™

Now available in trauma pink and regret grey.

Everyone is seated at a table.
A giant enchanted hourglass flips every 60 seconds.

"Welcome to Speed Integration," says Chad, wearing a velvet smoking jacket and holding a clipboard titled 'Hot Mess Bingo.'
"Today, you'll each meet former versions of yourselves and try not to scream. Or flirt. Or both."

Round One: Loki
- First Past Life: A 14th-century goat farmer

who speaks only in limericks.

- Second Past Life: A leather-clad interdimensional chaos bard. Smirks at Chad.
- Third Past Life: A sentient fog bank who once tried to seduce a thunderstorm.

Loki:

"This explains so much and yet answers nothing."

Round Two: Aurelya

- First Past Life: A librarian goddess who once banned emotions as "too loud."
- Second: A warrior who married a dragon and still regrets the prenup.
- Third: A gremlin-sized gremlin who screams "Don't trust love, eat glitter!"

Aurelya:

quietly: "Are… any of these versions emotionally stable?"

Chad: "That's not the point. Growth is the point. Also snacks."

Round Three: Gerald

- He meets his goth poetry phase (again).

- Cries.
- Apologizes to himself.
- Tries to kiss himself.
- Is gently escorted off the speed date floor.

Roarnan (the lion) sits down to find…
- A version of himself… with no roar
- A cub version… abandoned too early
- And finally a majestic, golden-robed version whispering:

"The name you chose is the roar you give back to the world."

Roarnan just stares.
And then… roars.
Not loud. But true.

Then comes Chad's turn.

Plot twist: Chad has no past lives.
Just alternate personalities… who all show up.
- "Business Chad" (suit, spreadsheets, dead eyes)
- "Crystals Chad" (hovering slightly, probably on kombucha)
- "Chaotic Chad" (the one currently hosting

this therapy group and who may be rewriting the realms for fun).

They all bicker.

Plottie gives them a timeout.

Final Line:

"Tune in tomorrow," says Chad, "for Group Trust Falls over the Pit of Eternal Doubt."

Everyone:
"ABSOLUTELY NOT."

Ready for Chapter Three:
"The Trust Fall That Broke Reality (and the Picnic That Made It Worse)"?

Chapter Three

"The Trust Fall That Broke Reality (and the Picnic That Made It Worse)"

(Subtitled: "I Thought You'd Catch Me, Not Trigger a Multiversal Collapse.")

Location: The Edge of the Pit of Eternal Doubt™

Brought to you by Chad's questionable idea of "team building."

A bottomless abyss that echoes back your deepest insecurities in different fonts.

Chad (with a megaphone):
"Today's activity is called Let Go and Let Plot."

Loki:
"This feels like entrapment."
Aurelya:
"This is entrapment."

The Setup:
- The group stands in a circle.
- Behind each person: their designated "emotional support catcher."
- Below them: swirling existential dread.
- Above them: ominous clouds shaped like passive-aggressive parent figures.

Things Go South:
- Thor immediately trust-falls with full enthusiasm and takes out two elves, a squirrel, and a casserole table.
- Gerald hesitates, whispers "This is how I died the first time," and vanishes in a puff of melodrama.
- Plottie jumps in backwards yelling "YOLO!" and accidentally tears a hole in the narrative.

The Realms Glitch.

Suddenly, everyone is in a meadow.

With a picnic blanket.
A basket of snacks.

And no idea how they got there.

 The Accidental Therapy Picnic:
   • Loki is now wearing a sun hat that reads "Hot Mess in Progress."
   • Roarnan is chasing butterflies while muttering motivational affirmations.
   • Aurelya is lying in the grass, trying to astral-project away from the group dynamic.
   • Chad passes out therapy bingo cards and a pitcher of emotional detox lemonade (which hisses).

Emotional Sandwiches Happen:
   • Gerald shows up with wine and a speech about vulnerability that makes a tree cry.
   • Thor brings his chickens in flower crowns.
   • The dragon eats half the dessert table and denies everything.

Climax:

A portal opens in the middle of the picnic when Loki drops his wine on a page from the forbidden fanfiction vault (again).

"WHO SUMMONED THE OVER-CORRECTING PLOT POLICE?!"
"WHY DOES THE POTATO SALAD HAVE A MONOLOGUE?!"

Final Scene:

The picnic basket floats gently into the abyss. Someone whispers, "I think the fruit was cursed." And Chad casually says,

"Tomorrow's session: Group Therapy Karaoke. Theme: Songs You Wrote About Them (Before They Turned Evil)."

Shall we go full ridiculous in Chapter Four: "Songs You Wrote About Them (Before They Turned Evil)", Karaoke Night of Emotional Chaos?

Chapter Four

"Songs You Wrote About Them (Before They Turned Evil)"

(Subtitled: "Yes, Gerald, Cry-Singing IS Allowed, But Only in Minor Key.")

Location: The Plot Thickens Tavern - Now Rebranded as a Healing Venue™

Decor: Fairy lights, karaoke crystal ball, and enough emotional tension to power a soap opera for five seasons.
The karaoke stage glows softly with mood lighting or maybe it's a curse.
Plottie is the DJ. He only plays emotionally devastating bangers.

Chad: "Tonight we sing our trauma."
Aurelya: "Can't we talk it?"
Loki: "Can't we run from it?"
Gerald: "Can I duet with the void?"

Gerald Opens the Night:

"You Said You'd Drink the Moonlight with Me (But Then You Bit My Sister)"

A 7-minute ballad with three dramatic key changes and a full sobbing solo.

Audience review:
"Moved to tears. Also, confusion." ★★★★★

Aurelya Performs Next:

"I Wrote This Spell Instead of Therapy"
A haunting blend of heartbreak, passive-aggression, and unresolved plotlines.

Midway through, her mirror self appears in the crowd slow clapping.

Chaos ensues.

Roarnan Steps Up:

"Roar Again (Even If It's Off-Key)"
- A simple, heartfelt anthem.
No drama. Just vibes.
Someone throws glitter. The Realm claps.

Loki gets suspiciously emotional and pretends he has allergies.

Thor Performs... a Power Ballad

"O Chicken, My Chicken (Why Did You Cross My
Heart?)"
 His support chickens harmonize.
The tavern weeps.
A bard tries to sign them to a record label.

Loki's Squirrel, Unsanctioned Entry:

"Don't Touch My Acorns (A Rage Ballad)"
- Screamed into the mic.
Stage-dives.
Steals Chad's clipboard mid-song.

Loki's Turn. Finally.

He struts to the stage, cape fluttering.
He adjusts the mic. He smirks.

"You Were Never Just A Joke (But I'll Pretend
You Were)"
 A sarcastic, sharp-tongued anthem with 0%
denial and 100% repressed longing.
During the final verse, Aurexia walks in.
In a cloak. With backup dancers.
And sings the rebuttal track.

The tavern explodes in applause.
Chad explodes in a puff of sparkles and says:
"Group processing successful. Next week:
interpretive journaling with cursed ink."

Final Line:

Plottie steps up to the mic and whispers:

"This one's called 'I Miss the Version of Me You
Forgot.'"
And reality shudders.
Because the Realms just remembered something
they shouldn't have.

Chapter Five

"The Return of the Forgotten Plot (And the Ex, You Thought You Killed)"

(Subtitled: "Oops, My Bad, I Left That Arc Open in Book 2.")

Location: The Tavern Basement... Which Is Definitely a Portal Now

The karaoke fog hasn't cleared.
The cursed ink from journaling therapy has started whispering plot spoilers.
And the emotional aftermath of karaoke night has made everything... unstable.

Loki (holding an empty wine glass): "Why is the floor humming?"
Gerald (clutching his tote of emotions): "That's not the floor. That's your unfinished business."
Aurelya: glaring at the inkpot that just screamed 'RUN' in Latin

The Plot Thickens… Literally:

Chad reappears wearing a cape made of therapy
notes and says:
"Okay, so. Minor thing. One of your previously
deleted subplots has returned. And it's angry."
Plottie: "Do we… feed it?"
Chad: "No, babe. You validate it."

Too late.

The portal bursts open like a bad review.

Emerging From the Rift:

The Ex-That-Wasn't-Supposed-to-Survive.
        • Has new villain armour made entirely of
old plot outlines.
        • Wields a weapon made from unsent
letters.
        • Is somehow hotter now???
        • And has a pet that might be a lovechild
between a plot bunny and a kraken.

The Realms Panic Accordingly:

Aurelya: freezes. That arc was supposed to be done.
Loki: pulls her behind him, muttering "Nope. NOPE. That's a nope from me."
Thor: throws a chicken at it. The chicken explodes. The villain catches fire and likes it.
Gerald: screams "I DATED THAT?!" and leaps into a wine barrel.

Plot Twist:

The villain isn't here to fight.

They're here to negotiate.

"You left me unresolved," they hiss. "I demand closure. Or a spin-off."

Chad hands them a pamphlet:

"So You're an Unfinished Arc: Rewriting Yourself Without Burning Down Reality."

Cliffhanger Ending:

The villain slams the pamphlet shut and says:

"Too late for healing. I've already published the
unauthorized sequel."

Reality glitches.
A crack splits across the floor.
Pages start rewriting on their own.

Aurelya gasps: "They've infected the Book Tree."

Shall we continue to Chapter Six:
"Inside the Book Tree - Where the Realms
Rewrite You First"?

Chapter Six

"Inside the Book Tree Where the Realms Rewrite You First"

(Subtitled: "Plot Armour Can't Save You from Self-Awareness.")

Location: The Book Tree

A colossal, ancient tree that grows books instead of leaves.
Its bark pulses with magic. Its roots hum with every story ever written.
And its sap? Ink.

The gang arrives through a swirling portal made of missed deadlines and emotional flashbacks.

Loki (brushing ink off his boots): "Great. We're inside a tree that writes fanfiction about us."
Aurelya: "I think it's trying to... edit us."
Chad (whispering to the tree): "Make me taller."

The First Chapter Falls:

A branch cracks and drops a glowing book.

Gerald picks it up. The title:

"The One Time Gerald Didn't Cry (And Definitely Should Have)."

He vanishes into the book in a puff of poetry and personal growth.

The Tree Has Rules:
1.	Touch a book? Relive it.
2.	Reject a rewrite? Lose the memory.
3.	Accept a rewrite? You may not like the version it gives back.
4.	Loki Rule: No flirting with your own plot arc. (He does anyway.)

One by One, They Get Pulled In:
•	Aurelya touches a branch that rewrites her childhood, but gives her the power she always feared.

•	Thor steps into a cookbook and emerges convinced he's a baking god. He names a muffin "Mjölnir Jr."
•	Roarnan finds the book with his true name… but it's been scribbled out.

The ink drips, then forms:
"Names are earned. Yours is coming."

Loki's Moment:

He finds his forbidden book.

Title: "The Version of You That Stayed."

He hesitates.
He flips it open.

Inside:
•	Him raising a family.
•	Him letting people in.
•	Him not running.

He slams it shut.
"Not canon," he mutters.
But the Book Tree whispers:

"Yet."

Final Page of the Chapter:

A storm brews above.
Ink rains.
Every branch starts screaming.
Aurelya turns to Chad.

"What's happening now?"
Chad checks his clipboard.
"Uh-oh. It's Editor Mode. The Tree's about to do a
full line edit."

They look up.

The sky rips open, and the Author's Pen
descends.

Ready for Chapter Seven:

"The Author Returns (and He's Got Notes)"?

Chapter Seven

"The Author Returns (and He's Got Notes)"

(Subtitled: "This Is Not a Plot Hole, It's a Character Development Opportunity.")

Location: The Heartwood Chamber, Deep Inside the Book Tree

Glowing scrolls spin like constellations above.
Every book hums. Every story shivers.
And in the centre levitating with far too much theatrical flair is The Author.

Clad in robes made of redline edits.
Eyes like glowing cursor blinks.
Smells faintly of burnt coffee and unmet deadlines.

The Author (booming):
"I have returned… to clean up this narrative disaster."

Reactions:
- Loki (whispers): "This guy reeks of mid-life plot crisis."
- Aurelya (to Chad): "What happens if he rewrites us?"
- Chad: "Therapy. Lots of therapy."

The Edits Begin:

The Author unfurls a scroll labelled "REVISIONS."

Each one hits like a lightning bolt:
1. Thor is reassigned as "emotional support jester."
2. Gerald is marked "too tragic" and gets a surprise disco phase.
3. The Lion is renamed Sparkles Roar worthy and given a tiara. (He loves it.)

Loki: "Do me next, I dare you."

The Author raises his pen.

But pauses.

"You're not in this version… yet."
Loki: "Wait, what"

A new scroll appears. Blank.

Titled:
"Loki: The Unwritten Arc."

Plot Twist:

The Author isn't here to fix the story.

He's here because someone else has been writing
over him.

"There's a second Author," he says.
"A mirror pen. And it's been rewriting your
endings."

The lights dim.
The ink shifts.

And from behind a glowing bookcase, someone
almost familiar steps out…

Aurelya gasps.

"Aurexia."

Final Lines:
The two versions of Aurelya face off.
The Book Tree splits down the middle.
The Author raises his pen.

"Only one version survives this rewrite."

And Loki whispers to Gerald:

"I should've stayed in the karaoke tavern."

Shall we keep going into Chapter Eight:
"Aurelya vs Aurexia: One Scroll, One Crown, One
Extremely Awkward Brunch"?

Chapter Eight
"Aurelya vs Aurexia: One Scroll, One Crown, One Extremely Awkward Brunch"
(Subtitled: "Please Pass the Tea and Existential Dread.")

Location: Neutral Ground The Realm of Slightly Passive-Aggressive Hospitality

Where ancient rivalries are solved over clinking teacups, forced smiles, and an unspoken rule: "No stabbing before scones."

A long table stretches between them.
Loki has already flipped his chair around backwards, like a chaotic youth counsellor.
Thor brought muffins. Gerald brought tissues.
Chad brought snacks and backup therapy crystals.

The Table Is Set:

On one side:
Aurelya Crown aglow, ink-stained fingers, and

eyes still reeling from a thousand branching fates.

On the other:
Aurexia Same face. Same power. But a darker scroll... and the quiet, terrifying calm of someone who's rewritten themselves on purpose.

Round One: Small Talk

Aurexia: "You look... exhausted."
Aurelya: "You look like you're about to monologue."
Aurexia: *smiles* "Only if you beg me not to."

Loki: *under his breath* "Five bucks on Aurexia snapping first."
Chad: "This isn't a fight, it's a metaphorical brunch."
Thor: "Metaphorical muffins?"

The Truth Unfolds:

Aurexia slides her scroll forward.

"This? Was meant to be yours. Until you gave it up.
So I rewrote it… better."

Aurelya unrolls it.
It's her own life without the pain.
Without the loss.
Without Loki.

Aurelya: "This isn't better. It's just… edited."

The scroll fights back, pages flipping on their own.
Images flicker: versions of Aurelya without her dragon.
Without the Lion.
Without herself.

Just When It Gets Heavy:

Loki fake-coughs loud enough to snap a realm.

"Ladies. Love the dramatic tension. But brunch is getting cold."

Chad stands up.

"Right. Everyone breathe.
We're going to do a therapeutic team-building
exercise called:
'Truth or Magical Compulsion.'"

The Game Begins:
  • Aurexia admits she once tried to delete
the Lion because he reminded her of her old self.
  • Aurelya admits she's terrified Loki will
fall for the version of her that's easier.
  • Loki confesses he ... accidentally kissed
Mirror Gerald once, but only to win a bet.
  • Thor says his chicken's feelings are hurt.
  • The Lion roars in lowercase: "rawr."
  • Chad summons snacks.

But Then…

The scrolls merge.
The brunch table cracks.
And a voice from deep within the Book Tree
whispers:
"Neither version is real… until one is chosen."

Everything shakes.
Aurexia vanishes.

Loki grabs Aurelya's hand.

"We're out of tea and time."
Ready for Chapter Nine:
"The Realm of Forgotten Endings (And a Very
Suspicious Map Written in Crayon)"?

Chapter Nine

"The Realm of Forgotten Endings

(And a Very Suspicious Map Written in Crayon)"

(Subtitled: "It Was Definitely Not Drawn by Chad. Probably.")

Location: Somewhere Between the Edge of Reality and the Back of a Very Confused Library Card

The gang finds themselves standing in front of an ancient, flickering signpost:

"Welcome to: The Realm of Forgotten Endings. Please Do Not Feed the Plot Bunnies."

The wind smells like lost epilogues.
A map flutters into Gerald's hands.

Gerald (squinting): "Why is this written in crayon?"
Chad (whistling): "It's called expressive cartography, babe."

Thor: "Is this a unicorn with sunglasses?"
Chad: "That's you."

What Is the Realm of Forgotten Endings?

It's where:
* Characters that got cut still rehearse their final lines.
* Unresolved love triangles go to sulk.
* Every "To Be Continued…" has a support group.
* And Loki once left three versions of himself here on accident.

One of them still thinks it's Book 2.

The Gang Encounters:

• A bard who only speaks in tragic cliffhangers.
• A villain named "Steve" who was too emotionally well-adjusted to make the final draft.
• A shadowy librarian who hoards unfinished musical numbers.
• A puddle labelled: "Here lies Chapter 12. R.I.P."

The Suspicious Map:

Chad points to a glittery 'X' with the words:

" THE END THAT COULD HAVE BEEN"

Aurelya: "That feels like a trap."
Loki: "Or a meet-cute."
Gerald: "Or both."
Thor: "I brought jam."

The Climax of the Chapter:

As they follow the path, forgotten scenes start coming to life around them.
   • A younger Aurelya runs past.
   • A version of Loki proposes marriage to a dragon.
   • The Lion gives a TED Talk on inner courage… but he's wearing a monocle and a sash that says "MISS PLOT 2019."

The terrain warps.
Reality flickers.
They reach the "X."

And instead of treasure…

They find a mirror.

A cracked, glowing mirror.
Reflecting every version they could've been.

Loki: "Well. This doesn't feel emotionally
scarring at all."

Final Line:

The mirror hums and speaks in Aurexia's voice:

"I didn't destroy your ending.
I just… took the one you left behind."

Shall we go on to Chapter Ten:
"The Realms on Trial: One Courtroom, Two
Aurelyas, and a Jury of Unfinished Characters"?

Chapter Ten

"The Realms on Trial: One Courtroom, Two Aurelyas, and a Jury of Unfinished Characters"

(Subtitled: "Objection! On Account of Vibe Damage.")

Location: The Grand Plot Court of the Realms
Constructed entirely from recycled exposition,
with jury seating carved out of abandoned
subplots.

At the centre of the room?
A glowing scale tipped slightly by drama,
caffeine, and one chicken in a powdered wig.
(Thor insisted.)

The Setup:

Judge Chad (robes, clipboard, stress ball) bangs a
gavel made from a retired quest log.

Chad: "Court is now in session. Today's trial: Aurelya vs. Aurexia,
Charge: Narrative Tampering and Reckless Rewrite Endangerment."

The crowd gasps. A plot bunny faints.

The Jury of Unfinished Characters:
   • Sir Broodington the Third (cut from a romance subplot)
   • Princess Rhymelda (a magical poet who only speaks in couplets)
   • Gary, the Guy Who Almost Had an Arc
   • A sentient sword who just wants to be held again
   • And Tina, a time-travelling tax auditor from a deleted dystopia

Loki (to Gerald): "Pretty sure I dated three of these people."

Key Moments:

1. Opening Statements

- Aurelya: "I never asked for the crown. But I fought for the Realms."
- Aurexia: "You abandoned your arc. I just gave it an ending."

Gerald: sniffs loudly.
Thor offers a muffin to the sword.

2. Exhibit A: The Scroll of Possible Futures

Chad presents a scroll that plays holograms of alternate outcomes:
- Aurelya ruling with grace.
- Aurexia ruling with power.
- Loki ruling... a tavern comedy improv troupe?

Loki: "That one's actually happening. Thursdays at 7."

3. Surprise Witness: The Mirror

Yes. The same mirror from Chapter Nine.

Mirror (echoing both voices):

"Neither of them lied.
They just… chose different truths."
Cue dramatic gasp from Tina, the time-travelling
tax auditor.
Final Arguments:
  • Aurelya chooses not to erase Aurexia.
  • Aurexia admits she never wanted to be queen
just to be seen.

Aurexia (softly):
"You had love. I had silence. So, I wrote noise."

The courtroom falls quiet.

Even the chicken takes off its wig.

Verdict:

Judge Chad delivers the decision:

"This court finds both parties… valid.
Resolution: Shared rule. Co-authorship. And
mandatory group therapy."

Everyone groans except Gerald, who starts
crying into Thor's muffin.
Final Lines:

Outside the courtroom, the sky begins to shimmer.

The Book Tree starts blooming again.

Loki (to the lion): "Well, that was surprisingly mature."
Lion (finally speaking in full sentence):
"I only threw up once."

Onward to Chapter Eleven:
 "The Realms Rewritten, But Who's Holding the Pen Now?"?

Chapter Eleven

"The Realms Rewritten But Who's Holding the Pen Now?"

(Subtitled: "Spoiler Alert: It's Not Who You Think. Unless You Guessed the Chicken. Then... maybe.")

Location: The Book Tree's Heartroot

Every scroll. Every story. Every ending ever told humming like a living symphony.

But the Pen of Intention?
It's missing.

Instead, a faint trail of ink leads deep into the archives... and something is rewriting reality faster than the authors can keep up.

The Mystery Deepens:

- Chapter titles rearranged themselves overnight.
- Side characters suddenly have main character energy.
- Every map now ends with the phrase "And Then Chaos Ensued."

Gerald: "That's not a destination!"
Loki: "It is if you say it with confidence."

Suspect List:

1. Aurexia? Too obvious. She's been writing poetry and helping Thor with his chicken army.
2. The Mirror? Trapped in emotional reflection mode.
3. The Book Tree? Sentient, but passive aggressive.
4. The Author? Still editing Book 2 out of spite.
5. Clarence? Is a lion. But suspiciously literate lately.

So who's doing it?
The Reveal:

They finally track the magical ink trail…

To a tiny hidden chamber.

Inside? A child's desk.
Covered in glitter. Doodles. And sticky notes with
"LOL" and "make dragon more sparkle."

Sitting there scribbling furiously with the Pen of
Intention…

Is a plot baby.

Yes.

The baby.
From earlier chapters.
Wearing a crown. Covered in jam. Writing entire
Realms.

Aurelya: "Wait. The baby is rewriting reality?"
Loki: "Honestly, could be worse."
Thor: "It's very emotionally advanced for a jam-
covered child."
Chad: "You know I told you to baby-proof the
multiverse."
Baby's Scroll:

The scroll unfurls, and it's magnificent:
- A future where Realms collaborate instead of conquer.
- Where dragons lead schools and goblins teach finance.
- Where plot holes are just portals to dance battles.
- And taverns host karaoke, therapy, and therapy karaoke.

But… it's unstable.

Aurexia: "Too many rewrites… it's tearing the foundation apart."
Gerald: "It's beautiful. And it's going to kill us."

Cliffhanger Ending:

The Pen glows.

The baby points it toward the group.

Baby (seriously): "Fix or fun?"

The Realms tremble.

Loki (grinning): "Why not both?"

Do we dare begin Chapter Twelve:
 "The Baby's Rewrite - And the Day the Realms
Became a Musical" next?

Chapter Twelve (Final Chapter)

"The Baby's Rewrite And the Day the Realms Became a Musical"

(Subtitled: "Yes, There's Jazz Hands. No, There's No Escape.")

Location: Every Realm, All at Once

When the plot baby slammed the Pen of
Intention onto the scroll, something broke.
Not in a bad way.
In a "Why is that sword humming its backstory
in perfect pitch" kind of way.

The Shift:
Music floods the sky.
Trees sway in choreography.
Chad's clipboard is now a tambourine.

Everyone… is singing.
And no one can stop.

Opening Number:
 "Welcome to the Realms (Of Overly Expressive Conflict)"
A fully choreographed intro where:
• Gerald does a heartbreaking falsetto about being misunderstood.
• Thor and his chickens tap dance in plate mail.
• The Lion roars in harmony.
• Aurelya belts a power ballad called "I Am Not Just a Draft."
• And Loki?
He slides down a banister mid-note, wearing glitter eyeliner and a cape made of sarcasm.

Loki: "I warned you. I'm classically trained."

Plot Escalates in Verse:
Aurexia arrives, singing in minor key.
The Book Tree starts rapping in ancient rhymes.
Clarence the Lion gets a gospel solo that literally revives a dead side character.

Gerald: "He was only mostly forgotten!"
The Conflict:
The Realms' magic can't handle this many overlapping songs.

The scroll is cracking.
Reality keeps modulating into higher keys.

Chad: "We need a final chorus to stabilise the
arc!"
Baby (conducting with a breadstick): "One more
song!"

The Finale:
 "Write Me a Real Ending (Even If It's Imperfect)"
A full-cast showstopper where:
• Aurelya and Aurexia harmonise and rewrite
their feud into a co-written epic.
• Loki sings a ballad to the audience: "You Were
Always Part of the Plot."
• Gerald breaks down crying halfway through his
solo, and the entire Realms sing the second half
for him.
• Thor shouts the final note with a chicken held
triumphantly overhead.
• Chad stage dives into a crowd of emotionally
healed goblins.
• And the baby? Takes a bow.
The scroll seals itself.
Peace hums through the air.
For now.

Final Lines:
Aurelya: "Do you think this was a happy ending?"
Loki (adjusting his cape): "Darling... this was just intermission."

Curtains fall.

Shall we now open Book Nine:
 "The Lost Realms Return (And Why Gerald's New Therapist Is a Pirate Queen)"?

Epilogue: Behind the Curtain
The Realms were at peace.

Mostly.

The curtains had fallen. The music had ended. The scroll was sealed.

But behind the velvet drape of dramatic closure…

Things were *not* quiet.

Thor sat cross-legged on the floor, gently patting Gerald, who was still sobbing into a muffin.

Thor: "It's alright, brother. Feelings are just… emotional protein."

Gerald: "That solo was in E-flat *minor*, my heart isn't *majored* enough for this!"

In the corner, Chad attempted to return his clipboard to tambourine form.

Chad: "Okay, so the multiverse *might* still be vibrating in a major key of trauma... but I brought snacks."

Loki reappeared wearing a very suspicious tuxedo.

Aurelya: "Why are you dressed like a game show host?"

Loki: "Because I'm hosting *Next Realm's Got Trauma* and guess who's opening?"

A chicken strutted past with a glitter bowtie.

Plottie climbed on top of the prop box.

Plottie: "Now that the Realms are safe again, can I have a sticker?"

Chad: (deadpan) "You *are* the sticker."

Meanwhile, Clarence the Lion was found typing a memoir titled "Roar Means Rewrite: One Cat's Journey Through Metaphor."

The keyboard? On fire.

No one stopped him.

Final, Final, Line:

The plot baby toddled back on stage holding the Pen of Intention…

And a sock puppet.

Plot Baby (to the puppet):
"Wanna write Book Nine?'

The puppet nodded.

Everyone screamed.

Curtain falls… again.

About the Author

Holly Symons was once told to write something "realistic," so naturally she invented a multiverse powered by bad decisions, magical bureaucracy, and overly dramatic crowns. She specializes in writing books that make readers laugh, cry, and question whether time travel is emotionally responsible (it's not).

When not rewriting reality, Holly is usually found brainstorming too many plotlines, avoiding spoilers, and pretending the chaos is all part of the plan. The Rewrite Realms is proof that she absolutely cannot be trusted with a metaphorical pen, and that's exactly the point.